Prais

"For fans of *Olive Kitteridge*, these beautifully written, intertwining stories will quietly slay you. Precisely detailed yet elliptical enough that we slip ourselves and our own experiences into the cracks and are at once immersed, watching the characters wrestle with familial and domestic obligations and making hard choices between lives of bondage or of freedom and transcendence."

— **Karen Essex**, internationally bestselling author
of *Kleopatra* and *Leonardo's Swans*

"In *Fate Havens*, author Mary Bess Dunn chronicles the despair of white middle-class Southern women who came of age in the aftermath of World War II. Told in a linked story cycle, the book describes the prison of respectability into which these women are born and how their impossible dreams are slowly blunted and tamed. As husbands, children, and friends come and go, can these women settle for the uneasy comfort of their lives? Dunn is a gifted writer whose insights pinch hard. Keenly observed and achingly poetic, each story sparkles with dangerous truth."

— **M.M. Buckner**, award-winning author of *War Surf*,
Watermind, and other novels

"Mary Bess Dunn's short story collection takes off in 1958 in a Nashville cul-de-sac, setting up the premise for the interconnected stories that develop through three generations of women. Dunn gets the Everywoman voice right: the things that break our hearts, the things that make our hearts race."

— **Phyllis Gobbell**, author of Silver Falchion winner
Treachery in Tuscany

"*Fate Havens*, an amazing collection of short fiction, focuses on Roslyn and her family, as traditions change, leaving some people behind, while others depart gleefully from those same traditions. These intimate portraits expose one southern family's triumphs and failures, loves and losses with a delicate, often lyrical touch that allows the reader to experience the kaleidoscope of emotions that comprise the life examined. Each story is told, not through the sweep of monumental events so much as with the smallest of gesture, word, and thought, surprising readers in the end with their accumulated and heart-piercing universal truths."

– **C.F. Stice**, author of *Always Yours: Memoir of an Adopted Child*
and *Darla Dreaming at the Carnival with Elvis*

"Mary Bess Dunn delights with sharp detail, unexpected turns of phrase, and richness of character and dialog. Read of women dissatisfied with the choices they have made, and of the men who love them. Their stories will haunt you for days and months on end."

– **Rita Welty Bourke**, author of *Kylie's Ark:
The Making of a Veterinarian*

"Exquisitely drawn tales of the fate we all face. Hope vs. reality. Love vs. aloneness. The desire to connect vs. the lonely human journey. Brilliant, insightful, and touching, Mary Bess Dunn's new book of linked stories leaves the reader thinking about the meaning of his own choices, her own life. A beautiful, insightful volume you won't soon forget."

– **Jennie Fields**, author of *The Age of Desire*

Fate Havens

STORIES

Mary Bess Dunn

LYSTRA BOOKS
& Literary Services

Fate Havens. Copyright © Mary Bess Dunn 2019. All rights reserved.

ISBN print: 978-1-7336816-1-2
ISBN ebook: 978-1-7336816-2-9
Library of Congress Control Number: 2019916346

Versions of stories in this collection have been recognized by or appeared in the following publications:

"Under A Different Sun" was nominated for a Pushcart and published in *Gertrude* in 2011.

"Color of Hope" was published in *The Smoking Poet* in 2010.

"Hats We Wear" was published in *Sanskrit Literary-Arts Magazine* in 2010.

"Storm" was published in *Folly* in 2011.

"Roots" was published in *Verdad* in 2010.

"No More Doing Harold" was honorable mention in *New Millennium Magazine* in 2010.

"Fate Havens" was published in *The Alembic* in 2012.

"What It Takes" was published in *Stone's Throw Magazine* in 2009.

"Certain Kind of Mother" was published in *Amarillo Bay* in 2013.

"Staying Alive" was published in *Quiddity International Literary Journal and Public-Radio Program* in 2011.

"Window Seat" was published in *Pembroke Magazine* in 2014.

"Closet Tales" was a finalist in the 2016 New Millennium Awards for Flash Fiction.

Book design by Kelly Prelipp Lojk

Publisher, Lystra Books & Literary Services, LLC
391 Lystra Estates Drive, Chapel Hill, NC 27517
lystrabooks@gmail.com

To Karen Essex,
who assured me it was possible

To Katie Gene and Barry,
for laughs and love along the way

Contents

Worthy

It is a fall morning in a Nashville suburb in 1958. Roslyn Hansen Meyers, no longer a newlywed or a new mother, understands that this house—their new house on a cul-de-sac of new houses—will have to do.

Roslyn wipes the bread with mayonnaise while the bacon burns, then reaches in her pocket for a smoke. She bites her lip, longing for the Lucky Strike that isn't there. The bacon spits as she moves it from the pan to a square of paper towel. She wants this morning over, but first things first.

At the whiff of Old Spice, she checks her watch, but knows it's 7:10. William strides in, so handsome in his suit pants and blue shirt with the navy tie she bought at Mallernee's for Christmas.

"I feel a draft." He frowns toward the window she's opened just a crack. William is a stickler for keeping the house closed tight. No use paying to warm the outside, Roslyn repeats to herself. She steals a breath of fresh air before reaching over the sink to tug the window shut.

William unlocks the back door and Roslyn watches him march deliberately down the drive. He walks without looking at the yard, where she's planted pansies and yellow chrysanthemums, or the sky, which hints at rain. She wonders if the neighbors think he's handsome.

William picks up the newspaper and reads it as he returns to the house. The kids trail in, first ten-year-old Ruth, her curly hair tamed with gold barrettes, then Billy, taller than his sister but younger by eighteen months. William joins them as they take their places at what he often teases is this strange round table she's convinced him to buy. He props the paper against the table's even stranger lazy Susan.

"Look here—they're coming out with a musical about the war. South Pacific!"

"A musical? Like with singing and dancing?" Billy asks.

"That's where you were during the war, right Daddy?" Ruth asks.

"My war was in the Philippines—West, not South, Pacific," William says.

Roslyn senses the children's interest in their father's war is strained, but whenever he pulls out the photos he took as an army photographer, their willingness to look seems genuine enough. Once she overheard Ruth bragging to a friend about the scrap of Japanese flag showcased in their den. "Daddy's souvenir," she explained, "the sun with a bullet hole in the center."

"Everyone eat up, Dad's dropping you off." Roslyn wraps two bologna and cheese sandwiches in wax paper, then packs them with apples in paper lunch sacks.

Finally, jackets, lunches, book satchels, and milk money are all in place. After a flurry of hugs and kisses, Roslyn's little family is out the door.

The house is not exactly quiet. There are layers of sounds, though none suspicious. A package is waiting under Roslyn's bed and she is puzzled at her own reluctance to open it. She stacks the dishes in the sink and grabs a cloth to wipe the table.

Through the window over the sink, she sees fists of gray clouds hovering.

She's just walked into the den when the phone rings.

"I saw the postman leave a big package yesterday." It's Mildred, the neighbor who's been in on Roslyn's secret from the start.

"Yes, yes." Roslyn wants to sound excited. "It arrived, but I haven't opened it."

"What? Why not?"

"Well, I wanted to see it myself before I shared it with the family." Standing before the fragment of Japanese flag, framed and sealed under glass, she begins to dust. "What if it's not what I'd hoped? What if it's ugly?" The flag's bullet hole, easily visible through the airtight glass, is rimmed in a crimson darker than the sun itself. Blood, she has assumed, though never asked. "I'm being silly. I'll go open it now."

But she doesn't go right away. She abandons the dust cloth, begins to stack a jumble of newspapers neatly on the side table beside the row of *Reader's Digests* and the small collection of aging literary journals received as consolation for her rejected poems.

Finally, she makes her way to what she thinks of as the master bedroom. She pauses to admire the room's freshly painted royal-blue walls, the four-poster bed, side tables, dresser, quilted spread with matching pillow shams, all in the Colonial style and all complementing her grandmother's Queen Anne chair. Though the room doesn't quite capture the homey romantic essence depicted in *Ladies' Home Journal*, it's getting there.

Roslyn kneels beside the bed, then reaches under it to retrieve a parcel about the size of her largest cookie sheet; she lays it on the bed. It was stamped with Special Delivery, addressed to Mrs. William Meyers from Family Tree Designs, New York, N.Y. New York City! Imagine!

You never knew what you'd find on a matchbook cover. Pocket games or magazine ads. Mostly drawing lessons. But on that day six months ago, she saw the ad for family trees: hand-painted on parchment paper, ready for display, large enough for the most prodigious family.

As she was often reminded, Roslyn and William came from kinfolk ripe with stories. Names. Faces. Places. She would hold onto their history by ratcheting up her mother and grandmother's tradition of displaying ancestral photographs on the bedroom wall. Roslyn's royal-blue wall would host photos as well as a family tree to show the fruits of every generation as far back as she knew and as far forward as she could rightfully record.

She said as much to Mildred, sitting on the front porch stoop, sharing the flyer she received back from the company, and going on about how significant such a purchase would be.

"Rubbish," Mildred chided. "You bought the thing because it's sumptuous—those fancy leaves and gold paint will add a little class to your décor!"

Roslyn appreciated Mildred's blunt response—even liked her for it. How was she to know what drove Roslyn to need such a concrete display of her family's roots? Mildred wouldn't know. She couldn't. As no one could, except for William, and even he lived as if theirs was a storybook romance. He returned from the war, they met and—after too few years of college, three for him, barely one for her—had to quickly marry. Things happen so fast, so heartbreakingly fast. The wedding expected of any Memphis banker's daughter was executed in short shrift, the move to Nashville—out of town—just as swift and just in time, for what could easily be explained, seven months later, as baby Ruth's premature birth. Ten happy-ever-after years ago.

She had to smile now, imagining what she'd say to William. Confiding how the moment she read the ad for a family tree she knew she had to have it. Yes, it was an extravagance, but he mustn't worry. She knew where she'd get the money. She'd give up smoking. Use the cash saved to invest in the family. Her little contribution to their future, she'd say, and he would shake his head in wonder.

Now she jerks open the top seam of the package to find, tucked in a cloud of tissue paper, the family tree of her dreams. The thick parchment paper with its delicately drawn water-color design is beautiful, but for reasons other than feathery leaves and gold-threaded boughs. Black-inked calligraphy heralds Granny Hansen, Papa Meyers, Great-great-grandfather Richard Lee Meyers—on and on, a plethora of names, relatives all. And there she is, Roslyn Hansen Meyers linked to William DeWitt Meyers, Jr., with their offspring Ruth Alice and William DeWitt III on branches below. But it's the sight of the empty branches—placeholders for what surely will unfold as her children's children take their rightful places in family lore—that brings tears to her eyes.

She doesn't mean to cry, but the weight of it all is hard to ignore. She holds the image up to the light. It will need to be framed. Captured under glass. She shudders, her fingers tremble, and then she lays the thing back into its tissue-papered sheath. Hands tighten into fists. She listens, hoping for a distraction—for the phone to ring or the neighbor to knock—any distraction will do.

It's been months since her last bout of what-ifs, but today, self-pity is impatient. *Captured under glass. Captured under glass.* The image resonates with enough truth to send her out of the master bedroom, out of the new house, down the drive past the chrysanthemums and pansies, across the cul-de-sac to Mildred's.

Roslyn wipes her cheeks with the palm of her hand, then bangs on the door. Mildred must come at once. Must see for herself. Roslyn's family tree is remarkable—worth the wait. Worth more than a heart can hold. Worth every Lucky Strike she's done without.

Closet Tales

Eleven-year-old Ruth hears her mother in the kitchen and her father fumbling around in the hall closet. She plunks down on the sofa, panting. She played until she got to bat, hit a home run, then biked the shortcut home. Now she all but forgets how the ball lifted over the pitcher's outstretched glove. She tucks her shirt into her shorts and waits, ankles crossed like nice girls do.

This morning, driving to school, her father said he would show them his pictures when he got home at four. She and Billy sat in the back seat; she felt her brother cringe. Their neighborhood ball game wouldn't be close to over by four. Still, her father didn't bring his photographs out often and always as a special treat. Ruth understood he must never suspect they didn't care. So, this morning, before her brother's certain moans of complaint, she promised she'd be home. When her father seemed to sit a little higher in his seat, she shifted her voice to just below a whine and asked—as she knew he hoped she would—if he'd tell the stories of his war.

Now her heart begins its whumping as the telltale scent of Old Spice announces his arrival. His eyes are small but potent; they glance instead of linger, and she blinks. "Ruth, you're a mess," he says, his face pulling itself together like a fist.

"Been biking," she says, choosing not to mention playing ball.

She watches the way her father's white-shirted sure-footedness fills the room; the way he sits down beside her, placing the yellow dented tin on the coffee table; the way he unbuttons his cuffs, rolls the sleeves to just above his elbows, then rests them on his knees without a word.

Ruth uncrosses her ankles and feels the nubby couch against her thighs. It is time to listen, though her mind is clogged with all he's shared before. Countless stories—or maybe only three or four. Stories of the house he grew up in, with the privy and the well, of how he enlisted in the army three credits shy of high school graduation, and how his best friend died beside him in the trench. So many stories.

Her mother's curtains swell with the clover and onion breeze of their front yard.

"So, where was it I was stationed?" he asks, tugging at the top of the tin with short but sturdy fingers that resemble her own.

"The Philippines."

"But where in the Philippines?"

"Manila."

"What year?"

"1944."

"1945." He grits his teeth, then doesn't. He holds up a photograph. "Here we have the hotel where they taught us how to shoot." He shot with a camera, not a gun. The pictures he took as an army photographer were famous. He was not. Published in her very own textbooks, his photographs—these photographs—credited only the U.S. Army. He refused to let her take the box to school. These were his pictures, he said. "General Shigemitsu signing the surrender..." He saw no need to share outside of family. "Tokyo Rose sitting at her mike..."

Ruth leans forward just a bit. She knows he needs her full attention. He needs for her to gather, to carry, to get his story right.

His voice unruffled, he continues. "This then is a geisha… this a prison camp… and here it is, a flattened Hiroshima." He hesitates now, giving her a sideways glare, as if to see himself in her reaction.

But Ruth is sitting, hands beneath her thighs, as her mind plods its way through all that she might say. The stakes are high. One wrong comment and, in the guise of teasing, he'd attack. Or laugh. Or leave. She reminds herself that the odds are in her favor. He's told her so: she could be the perfect girl, who said the perfect words. She could be so special if she tried.

She manages a conscientious nod as he adds a photograph of MacArthur to those he's strewn across the table. Empty-handed now, her father turns his wary eyes towards hers. She feels him hold his breath, waiting for her words. Hoping, she knows, for brilliance, fearing—no, expecting—something less.

She wants to throw her arms around him, but settles for an "I love you, Daddy" that comes up flat.

He smiles but it is not the smile she wants. She wants the other one, the one that puts her first. The one he gives to Father Joe at church or Mr. McGill at the grocery. The one he some-times gives to perfect strangers.

As if protecting the photographs from her trite expression, her father scoops them up and into the metal tin, then pounds the top securely into place with his palm. What can I do? she wants to say. Tell me what to do to make you happy.

He unrolls his shirtsleeves, buttons his cuffs, and stands up. She follows him down the hall until he turns and says, "That's far enough." Hovering there, she watches as he enters the closet and turns on the light. She watches him put the yellow tin back on its shelf. She thinks of slamming the door and then she thinks, for shame.

Ruth's bed is canopied with eyelet lace so beautiful as to make one believe a princess sleeps here every night. But not tonight. Tonight there is only an eleven-year-old girl lying between precisely tucked-in sheets, praying. The Memorare is the most beautiful prayer she knows. She found it in her first communion prayer book, beside the picture of the floating Blessed Mother with the veil. Here was what holiness looked like, and it was hers for the asking. ... *O most Blessed Virgin Mary ... to thee do I come, before thee I stand, sinful and sorrowful.* Sinning is the name Ruth gives her failed attempts to make her father happy.

But then it comes to her—reprieve. Ruth recalls how, when he turned to find her still hovering at the closet door, he shrugged, but his eyes gleamed. As if relieved—or reassured. Like he had won and she had helped him do it. *O Mother of the Word incarnate, despise not my petitions, but in thy mercy hear and answer me. Amen.*

Under a Different Sun

William was watching, and Roslyn knew why. She put down her trowel, pulled off her gloves, then picked a straw hat from off the ground. As her husband turned away from the window, she shoved the hat on her head and traipsed inside.

"Doesn't do much good in here," he said. They were standing in the kitchen, where chalk-white walls looked lemon yellow in the last strong light of this August afternoon.

Roslyn tugged at the hat's narrow brim, then lifted it off her head and returned it to the hook behind the door. "Hats constrict me," she said, jabbing at her flattened curls.

"With your fair skin, you've got to be more careful." William lifted two glasses from the cabinet.

She took his place beside the window. "Why careful? I've lived fifty summers in the sun—whatever fair was there is gone." She touched her forehead to the pane's warm glass.

"It's our ozone that's gone," he reminded her, pulling ice from the freezer. "This sun is different from the one when we were young."

When the phone rang, Roslyn tried not to smile at the welcomed interruption. She moved quickly, answering before the second ring.

"Hello."

"Hey, Mom, is Dad around? I've got some news."

Roslyn motioned to William, feeling her budding smile tilt toward resigned, then urgent. He set their drinks side by side on the counter, wiped his hand on khaki pants, and took the phone.

Roslyn walked to their bedroom to pick up the extension. She rubbed her arms as if she felt a chill. Over the years, Billy called from faraway phone booths on deserted roads, from frenzied bars in glitzy cities, or from the police station a mile from home. The sequence was always the same. She and William would listen on separate phones. They'd take turns offering just the right amount of sympathy and advice until Billy, his guilty burden lifted, would assure them of his love and hang up.

Roslyn sank into her Queen Anne chair and looked across the room, through the window and its interlude of fading sky. She picked up the phone. "I'm here," she said. While father and son sought pleasant ground, her gaze shifted back across the room, from the window to the wall surrounding it. She took a small breath.

With its framed family tree and family photographs, the wall was a memorial to her ancestors, as real as any stone obelisk or marble slab. Her mother and her grandmother had had memorial walls in their bedrooms, and they, too, had hung photographs in a way that left no doubt about who they were, (Hansens and Meyerses), and who they answered to (nobody). She scanned the photographs and found Billy's snaggletooth second-grade school picture—his heart-wrenching charm apparent even then.

Pay attention, she told herself now. Billy's voice summoned her back. Her eyes narrowed. Surely he faltered, hemmed, and hawed, but no, his words were quick and lively. She may have let a cry slip out, but she would not remember. All she would remember was his "Lenny," "love," and "partner."

Sunlight leaked from the room as she dropped the receiver in its cradle, gathered her knees tight against her chest, and cowered in the corner of her chair. She'd been here before, curled in its palm, driving back those who came to claim her quiet dreams. Not that it was the children's fault. How were they to know how much they cost her?

Some days, for no discernible reason, her courage faltered. She remembered Ruth three years old and Billy eighteen months, standing, staring, faces traced with tears her own had caused. Back then, her episodes had been cathartic. Sobbing—shrieking if the children tried to touch—rocking, telling them to go away. Afterward, she'd feel better, as if she'd gotten rid of something dangerous.

She glared back at Billy's photograph and began to cry. Hugging her knees tighter, rocking left to right, she looked at the photographs of Great-Granny Hansen, Papa Meyers, and Great-Grandfather Meyers.

She felt their shame. "Oh," she managed.

"He wanted to talk to you." William hesitated at the door, his arms outstretched, each hand pressing the frame as if it might collapse.

She looked up and saw his brows bunched with pleading. "No, what he wants is absolution." Bless me, Father, for I have sinned, she thought, recalling her own penance from the past: say one Hail Mary, three Our Fathers, and marry him, my child. "Can't he just be, be one of those...those...homosexual people?" She swallowed, remembering how she hadn't made a scene when he came out. "Does he have to announce it? Does the whole world have to know?"

"It's beyond me—this, this cohabitating, as he called it." William rubbed his forehead as if trying to calm a befuddled mind. "Still," he said with a resigned shrug, "it is 1978, Roslyn. A new age, or so they say."

"Tell that to Lee Anne or Naomi, or the rest of bridge club!"

"Maybe it's time someone did." He moved behind her, reaching over the back of the chair, cupping her shoulders in his hands—holding her still.

"He's asking too much—this is where I draw the line," she said.

She'd been a tolerant mom. Accepting Ruth's hell-bent decision to marry, only to wait eight years for their grandbaby; accepting Billy's quitting high school, running through a string of odd jobs only to wind up at Walmart, and, finally, his refusal to seek normalizing therapy. She accepted it all with silent nods, a neutral face masking disappointment.

She shrugged from beneath her husband's hands.

"There are some things that are still not right." She pushed up out of the chair and faced him. "We come from good people, William, these people." She made a wide, sweeping gesture toward the royal-blue wall of ancestral reminders. "That's your daddy's daddy there—he risked his life so we could know our Southern heritage. And my Great-Granny Hansen—she came over with the high Irish immigrants and worked for some of the finest families in Memphis. We may not be the wealthiest people in town, William Meyers, but no one would deny our roots."

"It's not our roots that are in jeopardy here, Roslyn."

"This is just not the way it's supposed to be." Her words arrived from someplace dark and small. "I disgust you," she said, searching his face for signs of retribution. What she found was pity. "Don't you look at me with that sanctimonious smirk. You

14

can't tell me the idea of Billy sleeping with this…this…Lenny doesn't make your skin crawl. I'm just saying what you don't dare." She knew her tone would do little to dent his composure, but still she turned away—impatient with his goodness—to state her case before the jury, framed and under glass.

"Billy wanting it doesn't make it right," she said, facing the wall. "What if I'd done what I wanted? Thirty years ago, when I had the chance? Had the chance to stay in college? To be somebody? What if I'd chosen not to mind what they might say—or what they wouldn't? But of course, I did—I minded. Our babies. This house. The respectability of it all consumed whatever once invited me to run—that's right, run—run like hell to keep whatever little dreams I had alive."

William stood motionless.

"You listen," she said. "Billy is an ungrateful boy. I cannot forgive him." She raised her voice above the roaring in her ears. "I'd rather he was dead—do you hear me—dead," she shouted, then realized there was no need. She sensed applause from the blue wall. "And to me—he is."

What does it mean to declare your child dead? Roslyn met the next morning open for suggestions, open for signs of how to proceed. The day was clear, warm with promise, as she carried a flat of rust chrysanthemums outside. Now she sat cross-legged on the patio's cool concrete, jerking up clumps of coral impatiens from red clay dirt that gave without a fight. She flung the plants in a bucket where they lay dying, bound for compost, their spindly roots peeking from skirts of sod, their petals brilliant still. She blew a puff of air from the corner of her mouth. The morning's shade had vanished; she almost wished for her infernal hat.

Not quite fall and, of course, it was still hot. She looked around at the havoc she'd caused. She probably pulled them up too soon, but Roslyn liked to enjoy chrysanthemums long before the first frost, and one didn't plant mums and impatiens in the same garden. That's what her mother would say.

The words brought to mind the lush landscape of her younger years. Her mother's gardens evolved from a row of blue hydrangeas and framed the house on Hembry Street, with plants chosen more for hardiness than show. Late April's purple peonies heralded summer columbine and phlox, while asters marked the start of fall, and the dark-green foliage of glossy Lenten rose claimed the breadth of winter. Her mother did not plant annuals. Their very nature—temporary and just for show—offended her.

But for Roslyn, it was the possibility of annuals that captured her imagination and prompted her to think about the lay of the land—not as it was, but as it might be. It mattered to Roslyn that she could alter her landscape with the flick of a wrist, a tug, a notion. It mattered.

Somehow, a year passed: days and weeks lived without Billy. Thanksgiving, Christmas, birthday parties, barbecues, and the Fourth of July—all took place without her son. What Roslyn could not imagine was how to forgive, much less forget, his betrayal. Thinking of him, her mind wound round itself like jasmine twisting on the garden fence. Though the lack of him was a subject never broached, not a day went by that she didn't imagine she saw him in the guise of passersby. She never spoke of it to William, or to garden club and bridge friends she'd known for decades. Tired at first, then weak, she abandoned her garden. When August returned, she took herself to bed, where she slept and let the summer end without her.

It was October. The hummingbirds deserted their feeders, leaving an inch of sugar water soiled with scraps of gnats and bees. Roslyn dreamed she and Billy were lost in the Smokey Mountains. He was three, chubby and proud, beside the girl she used to be. It was dusk, then dark, but they were not afraid. They slept, coiled, beside a creek bed piled with stones, and in the morning woke to find each other grown. Overhead the sun was high. Mother and son cleared the creek of stones the size of faces, then followed as its unrestricted water rushed toward home.

The sun she'd dreamed warmed the sheets and Roslyn woke up. Lying with her face turned to the wall, she winced at the glare of dawn on glass. A quick blink helped her focus on Granny Hill's moon-white pearls, on Papa's tidy mustache, and on the sepia-tinted photograph of Great-Grandfather Meyers. Taken in 1864, his uniform looked larger than his nineteen years. He held his rifle toward the camera, as if by handing it across the century, he might protect her from—from what? She didn't need protection. Then why was she afraid?

She stretched, and William, lying close beside her, touched her hand. "You cried out," he said.

"Look at your Granddad Meyers—nineteen and so defiant. Do you think he might have been afraid?"

"Nineteen is young."

"I was pregnant at nineteen."

She pulled herself to the edge of the bed. In the window-pane's reflection, surrounded by picture-perfect finery, she recognized the deadpan face as hers.

"When does an anchor become an albatross?" she asked.

"When you decide it has," he said.

She used both hands to lift the family tree from the wall, then shoved it under the bed. The photographs were easier. Royal-blue blotches appeared like bruises on the wall, as she took down the portraits one by one and stored them in a cardboard box. She saved Great-Grandfather Meyers's until the last. She removed his picture from the wall, then with a flick of her wrist she dropped it in the box and looked away.

Giddy. Free. Possibilities bubbled through her veins. Then the fear of flying, fear of drifting off, fear that she could—worse, that she would want to. This burden was different, but it weighed the same.

William found her in the Queen Anne chair studying the empty wall. "I didn't think about the fading," she admitted.

"We'll repaint," he said, nodding toward the lattice pattern of ghostlike patches.

"Yes, before the boys come," she said, practicing a sentiment she knew she'd need if Billy and Lenny agreed to visit. Perhaps by then her heart and head would find a common ground.

Roslyn went to William. They stood looking out the window at her garden, deserted since she took to bed. She followed his gaze across the landscape lying just beyond the wall, to gaps of empty dirt where her summer annuals should have been, where the mums should be now.

The day was growing. The sky was white with a sun brighter, less merciful, than a year ago. Luminous and frightening, she thought. A sun exposing more than she might have the will to bear.

Color of Hope

Lee Anne endured six weeks of comfort casseroles and widow's fare, then took herself out of the house.

"Ballroom dancing starts out with a simple one, two, three," Jan assured the class.

Lee Anne watched how Jan's skirt billowed and feared her own was way too tight. She was part of a small group of time-worn men and women with nothing much in common but the name tags hanging from cords around their necks. Jan pushed a button on the boom box and the students watched as she and Ardio demonstrated the waltz.

The man beside Lee Anne introduced himself as Arthur. He wore a pinstriped shirt and lace-up shoes that seemed to make him taller than the men who'd chosen turtlenecks and loafers. "Shall we?" he asked and held her to him sooner than she might have wished.

Standing eye-to-eye, she felt clunky in her church shoes, and her best blue suit felt staid. Through all the layers of wool jacket, silk lining, starched white blouse, and nylon slip, she could feel his fingers guide.

They began to circle the floor. She held her breath and set her sights on fixed points: one—a metal folding chair, and two—the wall clock, and three—the table where she first signed in. She and Arthur moved together, beyond each benchmark, to wider and wider spaces until the music stopped. She'd managed not to scuff his shoes, and a breath escaped. Along with doubt. Who am I to dance so well?

Arthur leaned in close. "What was that?"

When she didn't answer, he asked her if she recognized the waltz.

"It's ours," she said. Then she blushed and pushed away to explain. "Ours, like here—here in Tennessee."

He grinned, showing teeth that hadn't lost their shine. "Of course," he said, "the Tennessee Waltz." He spun her around, then flung her out at arm's length, and, tethered there, she felt her heart let go.

She thought of that first night now, while opening a package of control-top pantyhose and laying them on the bed beside her green chiffon. It was Friday afternoon. She had cleaned the house, fed the violets, and paid the bills. Only now would she allow herself to imagine dancing the waltz, the mambo, and the cha-cha-cha. All the steps she learned in the twelve weeks since Mike's death.

She walked into the bathroom, sat on the edge of the tub, and turned the water on full force. Tonight's class would be the last. Ardio and Jan had promised refreshments and live music and encouraged everyone to bring old friends to meet the new. She sprinkled bath salts and kept thinking. No old friends meeting new for this lady—her old friends would surely say it was too soon.

Deceit was never her intention. Every time her lifelong friends Roslyn and Naomi stopped by with casseroles and pies, she meant to tell them. She meant to explain how, eight days after Mike's funeral, a salesman called.

She inched into the tub. She couldn't tell her friends how she'd been crouched in her Mike's leather chair, thinking that from his chair her own chintz chair looked paltry. Instead, she would tell them how this man Ardio started into his spiel. Not wanting to be rude, she let him go on and on about how dancing was the tonic for what ails you—life's natural pick-me-up. Eight lessons for the price of four. He was so enthusiastic, she promised to consider his offer.

Consider it she did, experiencing a newfound spurt of glee in the process. She realized she wanted to dance, had always wanted to dance. Over the years she had asked Mike to take her downtown and find a place with music, even the Knights of Columbus party might be fun. But he would look at her with those weary blue eyes and frown. Slumping car sales, he'd say. Too tired, he'd say. And she would feel accused.

She touched her toe to the tub's stopper. Looking back, it seemed that once she gave up the hope of dancing, she started aging. So many years passed. Besides the thinning hair, the belly pooch, and flesh that looked forlorn, she lost her spunk. She started watching more TV and bumming rides instead of driving. Most often—dressed in shapeless shifts and house shoes— she stayed in.

No, she thought, climbing out of the tub, she had not told her friends what she'd been up to. But she thought they should have noticed just the same! If not her honey highlights or ruby rouge, at least they could be more persistent when they asked about her dropping out of Friday-night bridge. But good manners prevailed. No one pressed her for details, and by the time the lessons were over, she and Arthur had learned each others' moves.

"Feel the beat," he said, leading her around the dance floor with a grace he claimed was hers, and she felt light.

She dried herself and walked naked to the bedroom. Arthur had been a widower for years. As she danced in his arms, she admitted to him that Mike had been gone only a few weeks. Arthur squeezed her waist and drew away slightly. "Despair is easier, you know. Less work. Instead, you have chosen hope—congratulations." He dipped her backward before suggesting they sign up for future classes.

Maybe tomorrow I'll invite the girls for lunch, she thought, preparing herself with body oil, powder, and underwear the color of nude. I'll tell them about my lessons.

She slipped the green, gauzy dress over her head. She fluffed her bangs, took a slight breath, and moved in front of the full-length mirror. Rubenesque, not fat, with perfect ankles. She turned, but even as the green chiffon swirled around her legs, she felt the doubt. It moved her, this doubt, took her across the room to the bedside table where an antique pewter frame held Mike's photograph.

This was her most cherished picture of him. Fresh-faced and cocky, dressed in fatigues, headed to the war. She glanced at her watch, then blew a speck of dust from the glass. It was late. She'd better go.

The next day, Roslyn and Naomi marched into the dining room where Lee Anne was arranging chicken salad on china plates for their lunch.

"Honey, did you know you left your door wide open?" Naomi asked.

"Anyone could walk right in," Roslyn added.

"And look who did," Lee Anne said, spreading her arms to embrace her friends, wishing she felt something more than dread.

"Don't you watch the news?" Roslyn patted her chest as if to quell the possibility.

"I try not to," Lee Anne said, motioning them toward the table.

Naomi coughed. She'd been sneaking cigarettes for years. "I would rather watch *Wheel of Fortune*, but George is addicted to his nightly news."

"You never know what's going on in your own backyard!" Roslyn warned.

Lee Anne said, "Maybe we should turn the TV off and go discover things for ourselves."

They sat together at the table and Lee Anne poured iced tea.

"So, how are you, Lee Anne?" Naomi tucked a strand of short brown hair behind one ear. She'd developed a fondness for the details of disease and seemed disappointed when Lee Anne answered, "I have managed to survive."

"Getting into some sort of routine will help," Roslyn said.

"I don't think it's routine I need." Lee Anne chewed a bite of salad and stirred her tea. She was working on her words, in case she decided to tell them how Arthur had admired her green chiffon. The color of hope, he'd said.

"These things take time," Naomi said, shaking her head.

"What things?" Lee Anne frowned.

"Moving on," Naomi said.

"Moving!" Lee Anne sat straighter. "A body needs to move, needs to get the circulation flowing. Needs to dance."

Naomi shot a glance at Roslyn. "Maybe if I lose some weight… I haven't danced in ages."

"I made William dance with me once...on vacation...in Sanibel." Roslyn said wistfully.

I danced last night, was the only thing Lee Anne could think to say—but she didn't. She stood up. It was time for pie.

"I suggest you walk thirty minutes a day—that's all the moving they say you need," Naomi said.

Lee Anne set a cherry pie and her mother's heirloom pie knife on the table. Her heart was racing. Should she tell them how she pushed the couch and her chintz chair up against the wall and put the TV in the closet along with the rug? How she bought a CD player off the shopping channel and got the dance CDs for free? How she left Mike's chair right where it was?

"A morning in my garden works for me," Roslyn was saying.

Gardening. Walking. Roslyn and Naomi—her sensible, respectable friends. Well, so was she. Raised that way. Raised to know her place and wear it proudly. Lee Anne remained standing, her hands fisted at her side. Doubt had returned. Hope seemed a frivolous pursuit. What was wrong with her? The mambo, for Christ's sake! Her ears burned with guilty chatter. Who did she think she was?

Lifting her mother's knife, she thought she knew.

The moment they left she started cleaning. Baseboards, grout, the crystal chandelier—the more neglected, the better. Penance has its price—she cleaned for hours.

Two weeks later she was still scrubbing. She'd started on the junk drawer when the phone rang. As usual, the caller ID was blinking Arthur's name. She kept working. Rubber bands, pizza ads, plastic bread ties—by the time she dumped them all, the ringing stopped. She slammed the drawer with her hip. It was ten in the morning. Early yet. Roslyn would pick her up for bridge at six.

She started cleaning the cookbooks, wedding gifts she rarely used. Mike liked his dinners plain. She wiped the cover of her *Joy of Cooking* and thought of his last meal. Chicken breast, potatoes, and canned peas. Jell-O for dessert with decaf coffee. If he'd known it was the last meal of his life, would he have wanted something different?

She looked out the open door where green nubs of early crocuses dappled the yard. She set the cookbook on the counter and flipped it open to a recipe that covered one whole page. "Bouil-la-baisse," she read slowly and smiled. She liked the way the word blossomed in her mouth. She liked its rhythm.

She couldn't say why, but she stepped to the center of the room, slid her hands in the pockets of her polyester pants and eyed the yard. Then—thump—she heard it. Thump, thump, thump, she felt the beat. One, two, three. Her house shoes tapped the linoleum and her fingers fluttered. One and...lifting her arms, she embraced the empty air and glided past the *Joy of Cooking*, past the stove.

"Bouillabaisse," she repeated louder. Not loud enough, however, to miss the car door slam or Arthur shout hello. Just loud enough—she hoped—for him to hear.

Roots

What with the all-night rain still falling, Roslyn's room looks weary in the morning light. She's been back there quite a while before I go and find her on her knees, peering under the dust ruffle. She has on her suit and stockings; her shoes—alligator like her bag—wait by the chair, and I'm thinking it's the suitcase she's after.

It is the day of our son's funeral. At thirty-three, Billy's furies finally had their way. Roslyn uses the edge of the bed to push up and brings an errant earring with her. She clips the wad of shiny gold to her ear and winds a tinted curl in place. Her face adjusts to placid, but her shoulders hunch. She slips her shoes on, and we're standing eye to eye. From behind her glasses, violet pupils reveal the war within, and the voyeur in me cannot turn away.

The moment passes; she steps back. "Walls were never his friend," she announces. Her familiar matter-of-fact tone is reassuring. Outside, the rain dwindles as she picks a piece of lint off my suit, straightens the handkerchief in my breast pocket, and pronounces us ready.

The funeral parlor is across the river, in Billy's part of town. His partner, Lenny, has called with directions, his voice flat on our machine. This followed an earlier call. With Roslyn on the kitchen phone and me on the one in the den, Lenny claimed the detour was at fault. Claimed Billy was sober. Claimed the wall's abutment—where Shelby Bridge begins its reach—was not well-lit. And then Lenny promised to get back to us with plans for what he called "the service."

Ever since Billy died, I tend to dwell. As I fasten my seat belt, a high heat day when he was twelve comes to mind. Instead of trimming the weeds at the base of our retaining wall, he thought he'd burn the buggers—doused them with gasoline, then went inside to find a match, but the temperature was such that the wall exploded before he found one. What surprised his mother and me more than the rocks, stones, and clots of dirt colliding Armageddon-like against our house was Billy's reaction: had himself a boldface cry—spurting tears and all. Not that we paid any mind—if a boy's got to cry that's his business, but no use our condoning it. Roslyn did manage to hoist up a few stories of Great-Great-Granddad Meyers—fearless Confederate soldier when he was just nineteen. Richard Lee Meyers, fourth name, second branch on our family tree. Roots to be proud of. Roots to emulate.

The rain has gone back where it came from, but the road holds its slick. Roslyn drives, I give directions, following notes she scratched on the back of an envelope. Balanced on the seat between us is an old milk carton chock-full of fresh-cut daffodils Lenny hasn't asked us to bring.

I keep my left hand on the flowers and hold the scrap of envelope in my right. Once we get going, I stare out the window and wait for Roslyn to start her pointless chatter: tacky foreclosed McMansions, the new chef at the club, the bike lane that's more trouble than it's worth. But Roslyn doesn't say a word until we pass Billy's high school, and even then she reads the graduation dates off the marquee as if she is reading specials at the local Bi-Rite.

"Seems later this year," I say.

"Seems so. Maybe a week."

Billy would've been graduating about this time sixteen years ago, but he never did do school well, and instead of sticking with it for a few more weeks, he dropped out. After years of wandering he eventually got himself a gardening job at Walmart where he met Lenny. Six months later he called to tell us they were in love, moving in together.

Roslyn turns the wipers on low and drives right past the high school. I shuffle my feet, positioning them upright against non-existent pedals, which I proceed to push. The news broke her heart. She stormed at my chest with fists commanding me to act. She would not forgive. Not this time. Like a foot soldier dazed by his captain's charge, I told Billy exactly that, only more.

"Your mother is a proud woman, son, severely proud. I've known that since our early married life, when she used our bedroom wall to hang photographs of every relative—dead or alive—then spent more than six months' worth of cigarette money for that dang family tree. What's she supposed to do with the branch reserved for your wife? Your children? Tell me son, what would you suggest she do?"

I half expected him to laugh, to throw his arm around my shoulder, and cuff my chin. This was a joke. A colossal prank. But all he did was nod, first his head, then his chest, then his entire body. Back and forth. Nod, nod, nod, like a punching bag balloon who'd called my bluff.

"No matter," I heard myself say, "we've made up our minds. To us, son, you might as well be dead."

And so it happened that for a year—it took that long—we lived without our Billy. Without his belly laugh, without his spark. Even after we'd reconciled, when he and Lenny came to dinner every month or so, talk was hard. We kept promising we'd come to visit—have dinner in their remodeled bungalow—but these things take time.

A few blocks down, near the interstate, I read off the directions and Roslyn picks up speed. We're headed north. I switch on the radio. She switches it off.

There was the time when he was sixteen. He borrowed a friend's Corvette and, show-off that he was, drove it home. When he got to the top of the driveway, he somehow managed to confuse the gas pedal with the brake and drove right into the garage, through the freezer chest, then through the front wall, which buckled good. Best I remember, there were no tears then—a jumble of curse words, but no tears.

Roslyn reaches up, snatches off one earring, then the other, and drops them in the lap of her navy-blue suit.

I lean my head against the seat. Her lack of chatter invites my own. "Thought it might be the suitcase you were after. Earlier, when I found you on your knees." She keeps the old tweed case, with its leather trim and brass latches, under her bed, talisman-like, to store the family tree no longer hanging.

"Nope, just the earring—Gram's earring." She glances sideways. "Gave me a fright—the thought of losing it."

"I bet."

She glances down. "Even if they do pinch like the dickens."

My laugh is lame. Through half-closed eyes, I am watching a pickup truck in front of us struggle under the bulk of a rainsoaked blue mattress. The relief of Roslyn finally coming around to welcome Billy back in our lives was short-lived. "That's that," she'd said, patting my cheek before starting what she calls a new chapter. Saying one day I will understand, she moved out of our bedroom and into the spare room with its single bed and tiny windows. Sleeps there still. Seeing the mattress up ahead somehow brings all that to mind.

Against the backdrop of a pewter sky, the thing seems to be breathing. Soggy tufts of pulsing breaths rise and fall, and I am breathing accordingly when Roslyn asks for directions. I study the envelope, then slowly fold it in half and tuck it in my handkerchief pocket.

"Get in the right lane. We go east, over Shelby Bridge." Her lips clamp tight. I let go of the milk carton and am reaching for her, when up ahead the mattress has started to shift. We watch as it gyrates, then loses its hold to pitch up like a sail. Unleashed from the truck, it travels through space, slamming onto our hood with what feels like a vengeful thud.

The guttural sound I hear is mine as the mattress totters, there, on our hood, before somersaulting up and off when Roslyn brakes. "Shut up, William!" She is clutching the wheel and leaning forward. The truck without its cargo fishtails onto the median; the mattress settles on the pavement just ahead. Roslyn tightens her grip and squints into the rearview mirror before flooring the gas pedal and driving the car right up over the mattress. Kerplunk. Kerplunk. Our tires mangle the wooden frame and the metal springs; a blue-tufted swatch sticks to our windshield.

"Jesus, Roslyn." But Roslyn doesn't flinch. She keeps on driving, swerving into the right lane, making her way east, past the abutment and over Shelby Bridge, where Billy had crashed.

I sink against the seat. The milk carton is tight in my grasp, but the daffodils have spilled onto the floor. I stretch the seat belt enough to bend over, then take my time to retrieve each mangled bloom. I am wondering if, when we passed the truck,

Roslyn noticed the shoe-polished lettering on the back wind-shield or the passenger's white veil.

"Look here!" I say, shifting upright in my seat, a gold earring resting in my palm. Roslyn glances down. Her lap is empty.

She sighs like she does when she expects I'll know why. "Keep looking, William." She's released one hand from the wheel and is gesturing in a circular motion toward the floor. She's barely crying. "Lord," she manages to say, then flips the visor down against a sudden sun, "they do pinch, but don't you know, I need the pair."

Storm

Storms in the evening forecast had yet to arrive when Naomi saw the bearish figure staring through her patio door. She should have screamed, but there he was, squeezing his large body through the door George hadn't locked, to face them with the gun that maybe was a toy, but maybe not.

"Don't move."

His cliché made her flinch. George sat upright and his magazine slipped to the floor. He clutched his recliner armrests like a passenger preparing for a bumpy flight.

The intruder's khaki pants and spotless gray windbreaker failed to camouflage his girth. Naomi thought he looked familiar. But surely this huge man, pulling a roll of duct tape from his pocket, glaring down at her and George, was no one she knew. Outside, the first chords of rain commenced.

"Here," the man said to Naomi, "tie him up."

His twitch of accent took her back. Back to Kroger, to the befuddling coin machine where she stood with a King Leo candy tin full of coins saved from when she stopped buying ice cream. She'd been studying the instructions, fingers drumming the tin's iconic lion, for way too long.

Unless Naomi fixed herself up—brown hair and lashes curled, fair skin brushed with color, lips lined and thickly

33

glossed—she was not one to attract attention. But it was this man who, responding to her pleading glance, had parked his grocery cart and showed her how to key in her address. She'd patted his shoulder (a habit George loathed) and thanked him profusely. They poured the coins down the shoot and laughed together at the miracle transformation of heavy dimes, pennies, quarters into lightweight paper. Four hundred and eighty dollars' worth.

"I saved that money on my diet," she'd told him, her smile wide and welcoming.

He'd laughed again and spoken in his rich Hispanic accent. "Señora, you don't need diet. You are bastante...ah...beautiful."

Her face found its color, and it was this man whom she'd thanked once more, reaching out, touching his windbreaker, feeling his shoulder tremble as she squeezed good-bye.

Now she could only stare at the roll of duct tape in his large, hairy-knuckled hand. When she pulled the La-Z-Boy's handle, the back of her chair snapped straight, and the intruder jumped.

"Get up," he said, but softly.

Naomi closed her book, then pitched it aside. She stood up, checked her tucked-in shirt, and smoothed her shorts. She looked down. Her old house shoes were ratty. She slid her feet out of the shoes onto the braided rug. As the man held out the duct tape, only for a moment did she see his weary eyes and think, how sad.

"Do what he says, honey," George said. "Take what you want—the silver, the TV—take it all—and leave!"

"Wait," she cried.

She snatched the duct tape, then bent down and pulled off her husband's loafers. George's socks were damp with perspiration and smelled of fabric softener. How many hundreds of times had she washed these socks? She gripped his feet and wound the duct tape tight around his blue-jeaned calves and thighs, thinking she might easily secure his braided belt, his chest, his arms, his neck, his...

"That's enough." The man's curt command startled her. "Here, put this in his mouth and sit down."

He handed her a blue bandanna, stiff and new. She shrugged at her husband's wide-eyed stare. Then, as if he were a high-chaired toddler, she opened up her mouth and sure enough, George followed suit. She stuffed the cloth over his thick pink tongue, then bent and kissed his brow.

Still holding the duct tape, she fell back into her chair, putting her naked feet square on the floor. "What now?" She made her voice go dark, though the buzzing in her head was light.

The man lumbered toward the couch with an exhausted gait and his wild-haired head tilted sideways as if he had no strength to hold it up. In fact, if not for the gun he waved in the air, she could believe he'd merely come here to rest. He fitted himself onto the couch with the slow, gentle motion of one who was afraid it might not hold.

She looked at George. "We don't want any trouble," she said. But turning back to the man, she realized that she did. She did want trouble. She was scared, but her heart was racing like it hadn't raced in years. She set the duct tape on the floor, crossed her ankles, and cupped her hands in her lap.

"I mean no harm, Señora, I wish only to go home," the man was saying. "There is no more work for me here, and I am without the papers."

She uncupped her hands and rested her chin on her fists.

"Señora, please, I must have money to reach Tucson."

Naomi had read how folks paid a lot of money to be crammed

in airless trucks and transported across the border into the States, but she'd never heard of anyone paying to get out.

"How much do you need?" she asked.

He shrugged. "Four hundred and eighty dollars."

The man's chest sagged inside his windbreaker. "My papa is sick, he wastes away, praying to escape—praying for his son's assistance." He brought the gun to the side of his face, resting his cheek on its barrel. "The shame," he said with a hard stare. "I must take your money—or kill us all."

George's groan brought Naomi to her feet. "I have the money," she said. "It's in my old trunk."

Naomi glanced away discreetly. George would be surprised to learn she had such cash. She crouched down by his side, her hand on his taped-up knee. "Mad money," she explained. "In case we go dancing."

Naomi used to think that when she got thin, they'd go downtown to one of those clubs with bright, hot lights and bands that played till 3 a.m. She imagined dancing so gracefully that from the corner of her eye she'd catch the singer sending all the songs her way.

But when she lost the weight, nothing changed. Now in their fifties, she and George ate chicken at a drive-thru three times a week, went to movies in the mall, and then came home to watch TV or read. A fine life. Perfectly fine.

She rose, swept back her bangs, smoothed her shorts, and walked toward the hall.

At this, the man pulled himself upright to the edge of the couch, and, with one gigantic push, he stood up. Reminded of his size, Naomi faltered.

"I'm here," he said, stepping close enough for her to notice he'd shaved.

George bobbed his head forward, and Naomi followed his nod, staying in his sight while she led the man into the next room.

"This is my study," she said, gesturing for the stranger to enter. He stuck the gun firmly against her spine and she went first.

She switched on the light and let her eyes adjust. She felt the gun's hardness come and go with the stranger's breath. Inhale, exhale. Poke and prod. Could George see? Out of my control, she reminded herself, thinking then that perhaps the jabs were the random gestures of one whose mind was elsewhere. She cleared her throat.

The man shoved her toward a worn but polished trunk.

"Your money, it's here?" he asked.

Naomi felt his skepticism. "Yes, I hid it, under my skinny clothes."

He scowled. "Que?"

She bit a smile. How to describe the motley array of costumes she'd kept? Mementos, really, of the time before she grew fat. She looked at him again. "Clothes that got too tight."

"For you?" His eyes seemed to visit her body long enough to check a first impression.

She'd lost sight of George. "Same me, different version," she said. "I've recently lost a lot of weight."

As if to convince herself, as well as him, she lifted her arms and whirled around on one bare foot. The pirouette was unlike her, but then nothing about this evening was like any other.

"I'm Naomi," she said, "and you?"

"My name is Carlos."

George moaned frantically from the other room.

She turned again, only this time she smacked her raised knee against the trunk and stumbled. The stranger caught her, his arm firm around her waist. He held her steady, then grabbed the back of her head with his gun hand. He twisted her hair and yanked her within inches of his face. "You, Señora, are maddening."

She slapped him. Her palm tingled from the blow.

He loosened his grip on her hair and rubbed his cheek.

Naomi lowered her voice. "You followed me from Kroger. Don't look surprised—like I wouldn't remember." Her hands rested on her hips.

A smile escaped him, then vanished. "Madre de Dios, Señora, stop your messing." He unzipped his windbreaker and pushed up the sleeves. He was sweating through his black ribbed shirt.

The rain's now incessant pounding was interrupted by a shock of lightning. Carlos followed Naomi's gaze toward curtainless windows. "It's a bad idea, Señora—leaving yourself all lit up like this. Someone might be out there watching."

She blushed. "A worse idea is to let a stranger key in your address."

"Assisting you felt anything but strange." He took a quick breath.

Naomi could not disagree. "Here, have a seat." She lifted a blue daisy cushion from her dainty rocker and tossed it to the floor. "You asked about my skinny clothes, and now I'll show you."

She ran her hand over the trunk, pressing her palm into its humpbacked spine and brass medallions. It was large enough to hold a person, and in a way, she supposed it did. She pushed open the lid.

Carlos lowered his bulk to the tiny cushion on the floor. He raised the gun and wiped his brow with the back of his hand. "The cash?"

Naomi reached down into the trunk. She gathered all the clothes she could in open arms, then flung them to the floor. Two armloads later she looked up.

Carlos was kneeling, peering into the trunk, fingers resting on the edge. The gun lay on the floor.

"The money. It's here?" He lifted the King Leo candy tin, then tugged it open.

Naomi's gaze returned to the jumbled pile of clothes. She pulled out a bright flowery apron and wrapped it around her—twice. "This is as big as I got. An apron the size of a tablecloth, for pity's sake."

Eleven months ago, Naomi had tossed the apron on top of her stash of too-small clothes, then slammed the trunk lid shut—vowing not to open it until she lost all the weight she'd gained since starting this collection, shortly after her first wedding anniversary. Now she'd reached her goal, and as she tried to explain to George, it thrilled her to think of going back, with her new physique, to the pile of favorite clothes, trying on each piece, searching to discover what would fit.

"I couldn't throw them out," she continued, giving Carlos a quick glance. "As long as these clothes were here—these black pedal pushers, this silver blouse, these jeans," she said as she retrieved each piece, "as long as they were here to be reclaimed, there was a chance I might tame the beast inside that made me eat." She hadn't shared this with George. He wouldn't get it. He'd pat her cheek and say he loved her any size at all, so she should hush.

Carlos eyed the tin of money. "I think of the food in your country as a gift. My size—for me, it is a badge of honor." He traced his finger atop the lid, along the lion's imposing image. "The beast inside—it is good, no? Ferocious and unafraid. A blessing not to be ignored—or starved."

For a brief moment Carlos's eyes glistened, mirroring her own. She watched his face bunch and his body shake with sobs. This was out of her control. Nevertheless, she grabbed a yellow something from the pile and offered it to him as a handkerchief. He took it with both hands and lowered his face deep within the folds of what she recognized came from her trousseau.

Carlos gestured toward himself. "Look at what I wear today— clothes of a decent man. Still, I return to my home a failure. A thief who failed to bring his family to the promised land."

Naomi's eyes narrowed on the dress clutched to Carlos's face. "Don't talk to me of promises," she said, lifting her chin. "That sundress you're holding, I wore it on my honeymoon. It was George's favorite."

Carlos pulled the dress away from his face.

Naomi was rocking back and forth on her knees. "The color suited me, he said. Forsythia yellow—loud with promise."

Carlos spread the dress across her bare thighs. "I'm sorry, Señora, I didn't mean for this...I need to go." He was pushing himself up—one hand clutching the gun and candy tin against his chest—when the lights flicked off.

For a second, nothing moved, then Naomi sprang toward Carlos. He toppled to the floor and in the dark a loud crack sounded louder. Naomi straddled his huge chest and covered his head with the yellow dress to smother him. He began to struggle, swatting at her hands, writhing beneath her. "Be still!" she said, yanking the dress tighter.

"Please," Carlos said, his voice muffled. "The gun's a toy."

"I'm not a chump," she said.

"You heard it—that crack—the plastic exploded under me. It's a fake."

But the gun no longer mattered. She felt her pulse pounding in her thin wrists, her heartbeat finding its stride. Suddenly she was furious at him. "The nerve of you," she said. "What do you know about beasts? Least of all mine. Ferocious and unafraid— how dare you?"

His moaning egged her on. She gripped him with her thighs and dug her knees against his upper arms.

This was how George found them, his flashlight revealing a wild-eyed Naomi atop the seemingly dead intruder. "God help us! You shot him?" The light's beam caught her ferocious smile.

Ripped duct tape dangled from George's arms and legs. "What were you thinking? Have you gone mad?" He pushed Naomi aside and tore the dress from the man's face. Carlos's gasps were pathetic.

George rocked back on his heels. "You put us both in jeopardy, woman. You should've left this to the police."

Naomi showed George the remnants of the plastic gun. "A fake," she said.

When the lights came back on, her dress lay wadded at her feet. Forsythia yellow—wrinkled and soiled, but still full of promise. Knowing it would fit as well today as it did then, she picked it up and draped it over her arm. The dress was the perfect size—it was her life she may have well outgrown.

Brushing past George and Carlos, she took a few minutes to collect shoes, purse, car keys—and the King Leo tin. When she reached the patio door, she started to laugh. By the time she stepped outside, the storm was raging.

To My Son

The day I forgot your birthday, you would've been thirty-seven. It was raining the chilly rain of late April and the dogwoods had sprung loose after years of barely making it through the blight. We have seven now. Seven dogwoods that just this year have bloomed the way I remember as a girl. So, Saturday's rain was welcomed.

Your dad and I watched from the kitchen table. Maybe you remember the view. Our yard's pretty as a picture through the window. I made oatmeal in the microwave instead of stovetop, but he didn't complain. He's calmed down a bit since I moved back into the bedroom. Grief does tend to bring a person around.

So anyway, we were reading the paper. I read aloud and he listened. His eyes get kind of tired, so I read him the sports mostly, and the obituaries. I guess I might have noticed the date on the paper's masthead. But I don't remember that I did.

The rain quieted and the sun danced on the dogwood blossoms and I felt a bit excited. Maybe I could get out in my flower beds after all, grovel in the dirt, and get things ready for summer.

Well, then we heard a car.

And the doorbell rang and I looked out at the drive and recognized Florence's Caddy.

Your father had met Florence once or twice, but she'd never been to the house. She's such a cute thing, fiftyish or so. She lost her husband to cancer maybe two years now and moved here to be close to her daughter. She joined my garden club. Oh, the life she leads! Always gallivanting. Flitting to Philadelphia or Florida or Chattanooga for the hydrangea festival. Such fun she has!

Anyway, here she was on a Saturday. At our house, just showed up with no warning. Your father was not pleased. I had not nearly finished reading the paper to him, and he was still wearing his slippers.

But Florence didn't seem to notice. When I opened the door, she pounced right in and pulled out the ladder-back chair beside your father and sat down.

"Why, William, it's been ages."

To my surprise, your father laughed that cordial laugh of his—you know the laugh—and of course it worked. Florence carried on without suspecting how he'd be sure to ridicule her to your sister—her bombshell blond curls, her faded freckles, and her cutesy tennis getup.

She was quite taken with our table. Said she didn't think she'd ever sat at a round table with a lazy Susan in the middle.

"Why, this old thing? I bought it years ago, back when all my friends were buying square ones." I didn't belabor the point to Florence, but, come to think of it, I must've known we'd need the safety of a circle. What with the challenges this family has faced. Best met facing each other, not flanking. Even though you kids might've wished for an angle or two, that table did its part to hold us in each other's sights.

Florence cleared her throat. "I know today is not the best of days," she said, "but I woke up this morning with a nag of sorts."

She gave your father's shoulder a light tap. "And sure enough, I go paging through my journal and there it is.

"Roslyn," she says, as I set a coffee cup before her, "do you remember this fall, when I'd just joined the garden club and you invited me to help with the post office plot? We planted all those narcissus and hybrid tulips and you made the comment that they'd be blooming sometime around Billy's birthday."

She was pouring cream into the coffee, but she looked my way when I let out a gasp. The room seemed to wobble and my insides with it. I sat down and made myself look at the calendar hanging on the pantry door. April 26. Your birthday.

I folded the paper and set it aside before I looked at William. I knew it. His jaw was tight and his eyes glistened behind his glasses. Oh, Lord. Once he starts, it's hard to make him stop. He takes on so.

Morning stubble collected his tears as he squinted at me. "Now, Roslyn why would you be bringing up our boy at such a time, with…such people?" His voice was addled.

"Why, because, dear. I think I was looking at the flowers and bemoaning the fact that on Billy's birthday or on the anniversary of his death, I have no place to take a beautiful bouquet of narcissus or tulips. No place to go to talk with him somehow."

"Exactly," Florence said, slapping the table. "And you couldn't talk to that man he lived with—his partner. What's his name? Luke? Larry?"

I was looking at the calendar, but now I looked down. My oatmeal had started to congeal.

"Lenny." Your father had pulled a handkerchief from the pocket of his robe. He dabbed at his face, then started to clean his glasses.

"Lenny's had Billy all this time." Florence said. "How long has it been?"

I straightened my slouch. Forgetting a birthday was one thing, but a death day was something else. "Three years and four months and four days," I said.

"Since construction on the bridge caused him to crash," your dad said, the way he always does—as if the bridge was at fault.

I let it go.

"Okay, so for three years and four months your son's ashes have been at Lenny's…"

"In some tacky urn," I added, "on a bedside table—or so that's what our Ruth says."

"Honey, I'd say it's time to speak up," Florence said. "Go over to that boy's house and demand a cup of Billy. Just a cup and you could put him in the ground…"

Your father stood up. He looked bewildered and then mad, and for a minute I thought he might haul off and smack Florence—this was private family business after all—but he surprised me again.

"We have those plots, Roslyn," he said. "We could put him in the one beside our own."

I'd been pushing the lazy Susan round and round, but now I looked up. He stood in front of the window. From over his shoulder the dogwoods swayed, assaulted by a sudden wind.

"With a tombstone where you can lay your flowers all year long." Florence nodded her head at him and then at me, but your father didn't seem to notice. He shuffled right out of the kitchen and into the living room, mumbling. I heard the curio cabinet door squeak open, and I looked at Florence, thinking I should warn her to leave.

When your father came back, he was holding your cup, your

baby cup. "If we're thinking about a cup, this one should do." He was massaging the engraved, WDM, with his thumbs.

Well, he might as well have slapped me. I was that stunned. Your lovely silver baby cup— the one your Aunt Mattie sent from Tiffany's in New York City—was far too precious to be buried in the ground. I stood up so fast my chair crashed to the floor. I snatched the cup from your father.

"William, you can be so dense." I turned the bottom of the cup so Florence could read the engraved *Tiffany & Co.* That emblem said more than I needed to, and it was comforting to know she'd sympathize with me.

But she was standing now, her hand on the back of the chair, her face pulled tight.

"Why how silly," she said. "Who cares where the cup came from?" She patted your father's shoulder a second time.

Of course she wouldn't care. She has more silver than God— and bone china, too, with at least two sets of crystal. How dare she?

I set your cup in the middle of the lazy Susan, between the No-Salt and the Sweet-n-Low. Do I sound petty? I wondered, rubbing the hem of my apron over a newfound blemish in the table's wood.

What happened next might be more than you care to know, but it's the reason I can write to you at all.

Your father pursed his lips, then scowled in my defense. "Who cares?" There was a catch in his voice. "My Roslyn, that's who."

I looked at the two of them, William in his tailored robe, Florence in her awful tennis skirt. I smiled my usual smile, the one I use to keep my heart in check.

Only this time it didn't work, this time my breath grew

shallow and my throat filled with rusty sobs. I put my hands to my face and let the tears go, and then I felt your father's arms. I pressed my face against that chest of his. The one I had forgotten was like home.

Hats We Wear

I don't go to the steeplechase anymore, but when I did, I bought a new hat each year. Except that last year. That time, I wore the hat Yvonne had worn the year before. Black, tightly woven straw from Nordstrom, not thin and reedy like my Target brand. Her hat, with its swooping brim and single silk gardenia, was a hat of substance.

I was forty-three that May, balancing Yvonne's hat on my head like the dictionary I practiced with when I was twelve. As we hiked along a gravel path and climbed the hill with Nashville's finest, I told myself to pull my shoulders back and stand up straight. Yvonne and Harold, her husband of five years, led me past the sprawl of people sitting on the hill, past the bank of bleachers, through an arbor gate to our box seats.

Harold set the cooler of wine between his cushioned white wood chair and Yvonne's. "Ruth, there's your buddy," he said, nodding toward a red-faced, balding man in green suspenders and a straw boater hat. It was Senator Akins, as always, in the box adjacent to ours. Each year, in silent protest of his voting record, I ignored him.

"Morning, sir." Yvonne stepped in front of me. "I was just saying to Harold how steeplechase wouldn't be the same without you and that hat of yours."

He tipped his brim. "Why thank you, little missy, thank you kindly."

"Such a gentleman," Yvonne whispered when he turned away.

I longed to sit down, but we stayed standing to see who we could see and what they wore. The late-morning sky bowled around us like a glass paperweight. Voices lifted and fell. Hounds, darting between the horses' trailers, yelped.

The favored horse that year was Malcolm's Mix; the favored fashion, polka-dotted linen. I wore linen, too, but striped, and Yvonne forgave me. I was what Harold called her commie-hippie friend, the absentminded professor whom they toted along with the cooler or the knapsack of cheese and crackers.

I was used to being toted—to Harold's mother's for dinner, to Sunday brunch at the club, to the occasional charity ball. I told myself I went to be with Yvonne. We'd been friends since our first marriages over twenty years ago to crew-cut men who loved us like their fathers loved their mothers and couldn't understand why we were sad.

We left our husbands and pursued different lives. She raised Labrador retrievers, I raised a daughter, she sold computers, and I went back to school. We both did well. She made a lot of money and found a high-class man; I coped with mothering, taught teacher education, learned to kayak, and took up jogging. We called ourselves best friends.

Harold uncorked the wine with the deftness of one who played the guitar, wrote and sang heart-thumping music, read a book a day, and cooked gourmet—all while waiting for his trust fund to kick in.

"Chateau Margaux—shipped from Bordeaux." He brandished the bottle like a prize. Dressed in white, his blue silk tie with golden crests looked fitting. His deep green eyes looked brash.

"French wine?" I teased, pretending to be shocked. The American assault on Iraq had just begun and France had balked.

"I never let politics interfere with good taste. But the French will pay. They are nubs in the scheme of global rule, and they will pay."

"They strike me as a very moral people. I admire their spunk," I said.

"After all we've done for them, and they betray us in our time of need," Yvonne said, holding out her glass.

"Even if, as Dickens claimed, vengeance and retribution take a long time, the French will pay." Harold poured.

I was accustomed to his pig-headed opinions, though Yvonne's complicity still startled me. She and I once waited in the rain for hours to hear Gloria Steinem speak at Vanderbilt, and when we rode the bus to Washington to march for choice, we carried KEEP YOUR LAWS OFF MY BODY signs that Yvonne had painted.

"We might be the ones who pay," I said. No one seemed to hear.

"Cheers!" Harold toasted and we obliged.

The sun was low enough to reach beneath my brim. I sipped wine and worried about sweating while passersby I did not know stopped to chat with Yvonne. During momentary lulls, she pulled her chair close to mine and filled me in on the Alfords' ugly baby, Kerri Cane's Botox, and Jim, whose second wife was the spitting image of his first when she was young.

Occasionally, Yvonne would introduce me, but I preferred to watch. Thin and sleeveless, her polka dots a brilliant pink, her hat with wisps of net, Yvonne looked younger than she was.

Younger than we were. Her face, firm and flawless, showed pure delight with each new greeting. As if at last she'd found you, the one person she wanted to see. And though she did not hug you or grasp your hand, her smile was so beguiling you'd forgive.

Stiff clouds wandered overhead as a loudspeaker brought us to our feet to sing the anthem. Defiantly, suspecting our land of liberty of fraud, I kept my arms at my side. Harold and Yvonne had pressed their hands against their hearts, allegiance-style, and now he looked at me and winced. Damn if I didn't start to sing.

Afterward, as the horses lumbered toward the gate, their jockeys sitting stiff and proud, we cheered and I settled in. Yvonne scooted to the edge of her seat and pushed her sunglasses firmly on her nose.

"There's Kenny on Hell Shine and Jimmy Johns on Malcolm's Mix." She rattled off the names like they were friends.

Yvonne grew up with horses—the plow-pulling kind scattering the fields in Tennga, a border town where half the folks claimed Tennessee, the other half claimed Georgia. Her family owned the grocery store. They used an outhouse and sewed quilts. Yvonne grew up in Tennga, wanting just to leave. These horses, decked out with their jockeys, proved she had.

The actual races—the Bright Hour Amateur Hurdle, the Marcellus Frost, or the Margaret Currey Henley Sport of Kings—failed to capture our attention. Harold hailed a white-coated black confectioner who sold us chocolate-covered strawberries from a silver tray.

"Eileen should be here," I heard myself say. Harold's pristine mother was a steeplechase devotee who relished these berries and had been known to devour a good handful or two before any of us tasted the first bite. Too late to take my words back, I watched

Harold's bravado waver, his heart-swollen flesh exposing the boy beneath the bluster of the man. This boy was unaccustomed to his mother's absence, was perhaps expecting her to totter in, to take his arm and chide him for neglect. That she was tucked comfortably away at Richland Manor, where each day promised to be her last, was simply rot.

Harold's furrowed lack of comment was unsettling. "Nothing like a tacky remark from your commie-hippie friend to put a damper on things," I said.

Harold thrust one berry into his mouth and then another. I braced myself, feeling his state of mind take one more twist, the boy vanishing.

"Have I told you? I have an idea for a book," he said, unbuttoning his cuffs and rolling up his sleeves to elbow length. The book idea was nothing new, but my pained expression did little to stop its retelling. "The genesis of genders and the role marriage plays in warping nature's clear intent. Marriage is an artificial institution, invented by women to protect against obsolescence."

"More likely invented by men to protect their property," I said. I knew my lines.

"It has outgrown its usefulness. Men were meant to procreate—with younger women. Older women lose the urge to mate. Men never do."

"Speak for yourself," I said, shielding my eyes to watch the horses lift above the hedgerows and jump the streams.

Yvonne used a tiny mirror to check her face. "Go ahead, write the damn book," she said, snapping the compact shut. "For god's sake, write it and shut up."

"I'll have a chapter on good sex. The kind I had in 'Nam." Harold's eyes twinkled above a closed-lipped smile. "A lodge they called it. Very, very costly. Only officers got in. They served hashish and bourbon."

"I'm going to go pee." Yvonne slipped the straps of her high-heeled shoes between her fingers and walked barefoot down the aisle.

Harold kept talking. "They laid you naked on a quilted table not much larger than a cot, and when your eyes adjusted to the haze, you'd see them hanging. Baskets. Dozens of them, up on the ceiling, each one holding a young girl."

"Hush! You've already told me this story." It was true. More than once I'd listened to tales of his carousing, listened, I will admit, with wide-eyed fascination. "It's—it's barbaric!" He'd told me how the basket worked with pulleys. How the bottom opened and the girl was lowered on a harness he controlled.

I glanced away from the track. Harold had moved. He sat beside me. When everyone around us started standing, we sat still. It was the crowd's collective gasp that I remember as he leaned in close and kissed me hard.

"I've wanted to do that for a long time," he said, pulling away, knocking my hat awry. Around us an unsettling murmur rippled through the crowd. We had to stand to see the horse. Dead. Torso twisted around a bend in the track, legs sprawled backward, with neck and handsome face skewed toward the sky.

After the races, inside the patrons' tent, no one chose to talk of Malcolm's Mix. How he broke his back. How his jockey walked away, unharmed. It was a party, after all. Cloth-covered tables, more cushioned chairs. Yellow roses in crystal vases. A band played '60s music. There was food.

Yvonne and I set our glasses on a table and walked toward

the buffet. I tried to follow her through the crowd, but the wine's effects slowed me down. Strangers jostled me. It was warm, but I suspect the hot I felt was the hot of not belonging.

I caught the smell of steaming beef. "Dr. Meyers." The crowd shuffled forward. "Dr. Meyers." The voice came from the other side of the buffet table. The servers' side. I scanned a line of white-coated men and women. All of them black, one of them familiar.

"Jimmy Ray. Hey, how are you?" I talked as if no table stood between us. As if there were no others prodding me along, waving plates before him, giving orders he acknowledged with a nod. I stepped out of line and waited. Jimmy was a graduate student in my Schools and Social Justice class. As I watched him lifting tenderloin slices and scooping up potatoes, it occurred to me I'd been outed.

"Looking fine there, Doc."

"Yeah, well, I clean up real good." I nodded, and my hat wobbled.

"What can I get you here?" It was his turn to ignore what lay between us.

"The pork loin looks tasty and whatever else you'd recommend."

"Sorry, Doc, I can't recommend a thing. They don't let us eat. We're here to serve."

"This your weekend gig?" I laughed and held out my plate.

"Is it yours?" He almost smiled, as he placed the meat, roasted peppers, and tomato salad on the plate with care.

"My friends," I lied, "insisted that I come." I looked down at my plate. The food was artfully arranged. Presentation is all, Harold would say. "Nice job," I said to Jimmy, knowing I'd said the same to him in class.

He caught my eye and then gave a quick salute before turning his attention to other guests.

Plate in hand, I wandered back to our table and was glad to find Yvonne alone.

"One of my students is here." I sat down. "Jimmy Ray."

"Here?" She looked around.

"Serving," I said.

"My hat looks good on you."

"I'm not comfortable in hats."

"It's not about comfort, is it?"

"Isn't it?" Now I glanced around. "Everything here reeks of it."

"Well, is that so terrible?"

"I worry comfort numbs."

"Sometimes numbing is a salve." She was annoyed. "Do you always have to look at the underside of things? Besides, it's not easy to be a part of all of this; it takes work."

"Yes, I know." I shook my head. "I've seen how it consumes you."

She was staring at my plate. "You didn't get any lemon squares," she said and gave me one of hers. "Look, we're being paged." She nodded at Harold, who was gesturing for us to join him on the dance floor.

"In a minute," I said and watched her go. It occurred to me I might slip away. Take off my hat, leave it on the padded chair, and run. I'd carry my high heels and wave at Jimmy, just so he would know I hadn't stayed. I took a bite of lukewarm pork. It wasn't good to sit alone. You think too much, Yvonne would say whenever I was moody.

"Ruth, Ruth Meyers?" A small-boned man bent down and squinted. "I didn't recognize you without your helmet."

I smiled at Scott. We often kayaked together. "I needed a different kind of hat today. These are rapids of another sort."

"You two going to sit there gabbing? It's a party, goddamn it." Harold hollered at us from the edge of the dance floor where he and Yvonne were gyrating to "In the Midnight Hour."

"Shall we?" Scott asked.

"We shall," I said, welcoming the hand he offered.

The band was loud but the crowd was louder. Everyone was singing lyrics like they'd sung them years ago. With different partners, in different settings, but the music and the lyrics were the same. Yesterday's music. Our yesterdays. The kind that entered you and stayed.

On the dance floor, Scott and I raised our arms to the chorus. I kicked my shoes off, tossed the hat, and fluffed my hair. We were singing out loud when I caught sight of Jimmy scraping dishes. He stacked up wine glasses and dropped lipstick-blotted napkins in a pile. Yvonne danced in her husband's arms. I waved at them like I was having fun. As the band played one last refrain, Scott twirled me around, and then dizzy from the effort, I stood still. The buffet table had been cleared away. It was time to go.

I said goodbye to Scott and started down the hill with Yvonne and Harold. I don't remember that we said a word, even when we passed the sheet-covered bulk of Malcolm Mix.

Harold had driven halfway home when he looked into the rearview mirror and caught my eye.

"I hear your buddy, the senator, got into a spat over dinner. Seems he was going through the buffet line and one of the servers started in on him for supporting corporate tax breaks.

Senator Akins said the boy kept going on and on." Harold shook his head and chuckled. "Uppity was the word he used. The kid was downright uppity."

Too tired to argue, I rolled down the window and shifted out of view of Harold's dark eyes. It felt good to settle against the opulent leather seat. It was dusk. The moon was waiting. And I remember I was happy. The happy of swallowing a splendid pear and knowing more are piled upon the plate. And I was cared for. Yvonne and Harold loved me, probably. Their willingness—no, insistence—that I accompany them from one event to the next—events bursting with good taste—demanded nothing from me but devotion.

I'd managed to salvage Yvonne's hat from the dance floor and now, as the air slapped my face, I worked to smooth the tainted silk gardenia back in shape.

A year later they are living in a resort community outside Santa Fe. The sky, they assure me, is wide and bright, unlike any I had ever seen. Dazzling. "You must come. We have an extra room." I do intend to visit. That I have not plagues this shining May day with the unsettled sense that I am missing out. As if the party's going on without me but I have no clothes. Nothing to wear. Everything I own is way too drab.

Fate Havens

Roslyn arrives at Colors late. Her hair, a tangled mess, shows little evidence of last week's appointment. "Traffic on the Fate Havens is snarled," she says, then inhales loudly, pausing to look calm, though she wants to cheer. She's arrived! Driven herself here without a single mishap. Wonders.

"That bridge—such a sorry state," Sylvie, the receptionist, covers the phone's receiver with her palm.

A breath of permanent solution, a whiff of talc, the salon's potpourri of the newest gels and old-time sprays shift into focus. Dryers hang from hooks at mirrored stations where Mark, Joann, and Caroline tart up faithful customers in swivel chairs. The shampoo girl, Nicky, flits between her loose-lipped sinks, carrying a hot-wax bowl poised atop a stack of folded towels.

Roslyn hurries into the dressing room where she hopes to find a magenta smock that snaps. There are no magenta smocks, only three gray ones that tie. She shakes her head, knots the gray sash, and steps into the salon. In unison, Nicky and Mark call out to her with "Hey there!" and "How you do?"

After all these years of regular two o'clock Saturday appointments, Mark and Nicky have come to hold a special place in Roslyn's heart. The fact that she can talk to one or the other about whatever crosses her mind is worth more than having hair that holds its curl. Especially this year, or however long it's been, since Roslyn caught Mark's eye in the mirror and confessed.

"I am not the person I used to be."

"Who is?" Nicky, whose black nail polish and random tattoos belied her years, chimed in.

Mark shook his head at Nicky. "Why say that?" he asked Roslyn.

"William tells me I'm forgetting," she said. "Says I repeat myself. Same story twice or three times in an afternoon."

The next week she had drummed her fingers on the arm of Mark's chair while relating how she'd been driving William to Arby's for lunch, but they ended up at Captain D's instead. "Now he's all a-twitter, afraid I'll be driving and forget where I am or where I'm going."

"Ridiculous," Mark mumbled, or so she thought.

Next thing she had to tell them was, William took her keys. "He claims to enjoy toting me around." Roslyn rolled her eyes. "There's this commercial…about the vanishing mind…"

Mark switched the dryer to high. When he finished, Roslyn was exclaiming, "Ha! The Roslyn that you know might soon be empty of the everyday. Empty, but demanding care." Roslyn couldn't stand the thought, she insisted to Nicky. "I'm not the one who will suffer. William is the one who'll have to pay."

A month later, when Nicky remarked on Roslyn's red-rimmed eyes, she sat in the chair and wept. On their way to her appointment with a brain specialist, William had collapsed. He was dying, Roslyn sputtered, yet all she could feel was relief.

This twist of fate, cruel as it was, nonetheless ensured whatever burden she would be, would not be William's.

"I read they were going to start working on that bridge. Something about the guard rails being way too low," Caroline is saying as she trims her customer's bangs.

Roslyn slides her backside to the front of the shampoo chair, stretching out to rest her neck against the sink.

"What's that?" Nicky is leaning over Roslyn. "That tune. Did I hear you humming?"

Roslyn blushes. Humming was a private affair.

"Well, whatever," Nicky says without waiting for a response, "it's perky, I like it." She adjusts the faucet, her tattooed underarm flashing into view.

"Nice rose," Roslyn says. She cups her hands in her lap and stares, as she always does, at the ceiling where Mark has painted palm trees, sail boats, and half-dressed ladies with wide open eyes.

"Nothing but an invitation if you ask me," Sylvie says.

"The bridge?" Caroline asks from her station across the room.

Sylvie nods. "Damaged souls are quick to take the plunge."

Roslyn is determined not to hum. For days now, without warning, tunes have been slipping out from between her lips—unfamiliar, "perky" tunes.

The women on the ceiling are not young or dainty or even beautiful, but they stand with bare feet planted in the sand, fists on hips, breasts spilling from halter-tops. She remembers a sandy beach at Rainbow Lake, with pine trees instead of palm, where she and her friends caused quite a stir in halter tops much like these floating in the ceiling scene above.

Roslyn closes her eyes. Are beaches out of the question? They'd travelled to Sanibel Island ages ago. But William's no longer fond of sand. Or sweat. Or people, for that matter. People wear him out, make it hard to relax. She is all he needs. He is happiest with just the two of them—when he doesn't have to entertain. Or speak. Her friends envy such devotion. But lately, in her worst moments, Roslyn fears William might secretly relish the idea of her illness, the idea of her actually becoming what he's always endearingly called her: his pet.

But no. William is about to die. She's left him at the hospital, in intensive care, with tubes sprouting and numbers glowing from baffling machines that wink his fate.

She's left him with the day nurse, Betty. William likes Betty. He's discovered she went to Memphis State and stayed in Furman Hall like Roslyn. The coincidence is what he's latched onto, what he can share in the ten minutes visitors are allowed to stay. In spite of the tube climbing out of his mouth over his shoulder into the bag hanging from the hook above his head, William feels he must amuse. The coincidence of Nurse Betty and his wife Roslyn sharing the same school and the same dorm, though decades apart, is conveyed more than once. "Course a looker like my Roslyn, why, I plucked her up and out of there in nothing flat. Couldn't chance her setting sights on anyone—or anything—but me." By the end of William's story, time is up and visitors, supplied with one good anecdote, can leave.

The faucet gushes. Roslyn hopes the water will be very hot. She feels Nicky's fingers and hopes she'll rub hard and long and knead both temples. She does not, and the water turns tepid by the final rinse. "All done!" Nicky chirps. Roslyn's "Thanks" is flat.

In Mark's chair, she adjusts the plastic smock tighter over her cleavage.

Mark's "And? How are you?" demands no reply, for he brandishes the canister of amber dye and begins to squirt. It is cold on her scalp and trickles down the side of her face. Using the smock's sleeve, she dabs at the wayward dye and when she does, something moves inside of her. A familiar something, slippery as a dream, but not as harmless.

She looks into the mirror at her wet-rat self, with her lazy skin and her lips too thin to matter. She blinks behind her glasses and finds Mark's gaze.

"If William dies tonight, I will not go to church in the morning."

She waits for something to happen. Some sign that she has contaminated the air—adding the fumes of sin to its fumes of peroxide and bleach. It occurs to her there's more where that came from, more wicked threats—to drive for days, to get her backside tattooed, to scream.

Mark spreads the dye with gloved fingers. "Well, Roslyn, dear, that might not be such a bad idea. If William dies, you'll probably have more on your plate than Sunday church."

But Roslyn is not listening. She is back at Rainbow Lake, stretched out, perched on her hip in the sand, Aphrodite-like. She is seventeen, with a gift for words, for style. An acceptance letter—all the way from Chicago—waits at home on the dressing table beside the notebook and the silver combs.

"Your glasses," Mark says, and she removes them.

How did this happen? This life and not another?

She settles deep into the swivel chair. Mark is saying how he stopped going to church ages ago. "These days, painting is what feeds my soul."

Again, Roslyn squints, and with a soft "Lucky you," escapes back to her lake, her letter, and her seventeen-year-old self. But the scene clouds. She sways forward, willing the girl to return. What comes to mind is her father's common sense: No use your gallivanting up north, State is as fine a school as any.

"Roslyn, Roslyn honey." Sylvie's voice is tender. "Phone."

The salon falls silent while Roslyn slips on her glasses, pushes out of the chair, scans her mirrored self, and gently nods. The familiar something moves again, only this time it is more insistent. It pushes her across the room, sifting inside her, becoming more tangible, becoming more like what she used to think of as desire. She swallows a hum.

Sylvie hands Roslyn the phone.

"I'm ready," she says into the receiver. She grips the knot at her waist. "I see," she says. "I see," she says again, glaring now at the salon's red door. "A miracle? Why, yes, of course. I see."

She reaches over the desk and sets the receiver in its cradle. Her clucking tongue is loud against respectful silence. She turns, lifts her chin, and says, to no one in particular, "He's going to live."

Sylvie is the first to reach her with a hug. Mark, Joann, and Caroline follow suit. Roslyn stands, patiently accepting their goodwill.

"Okay, okay," she says at last, "guess I'd better get on with things."

Only Nicky has yet to speak, and when she gestures toward the bowl of hot wax, her voice registers concern. "You ready for me?"

"Sure." Making her way past the much too bright windows, Roslyn takes her place in Nicky's chair.

"You still with us?" Nicky leans closer to Roslyn, who, even as she fingers the space above her lip, seizes on the implications of Sylvia's earlier remarks. of what's been said.

"Sorry," Roslyn shrugs, recognizing in the Fate Havens, with its low rails and easy access, an invitation to change what is happening to this damaged soul. Nicky holds the bowl in one palm and uses a flat wooden applicator to stir until Roslyn lifts her face, wide-eyed, to catch the wax.

The notion she might do it, might actually drive through the guardrail—sets her pulse to racing. In the salon's back parking lot, her silver-blue Pontiac looks as regal as it used to make her feel. She marches past taller, boxier cars, opens her door, and slides behind the wheel. From the rearview mirror, she sees her hair is nice, the color of caramel, fixed so as to add a little height. She turns on the ignition and backs out onto Magnolia Street, which takes her to Tyne then right out Highway 4. Fate Havens is up ahead.

Roslyn guns the motor, trying to decide if she should raise or lower the windows before taking the plunge. William would know. It always surprised her, the sorts of minutia he tucked away in that head of his.

She grips the steering wheel, and her gaze falls on St. Christopher, patron saint of travelers. She snatches the small statue off the dash—a gift from William, years ago. Her heart slows. He gave it to her for luck. She won the local round of radio's *Winner Take All*, then went to Chicago for the finals. She didn't win, of course. But William was proud. He made her buy a new outfit and told everyone they knew of Roslyn's fame.

Now she stops the Pontiac at a small convenience market close to the foot of the bridge. She parks on the side and sits in the car, studying the store windows smattered with ads for slushies, cigarettes, and giant drinks. She takes the keys out of the ignition, stuffs her purse under the seat, gets out of the car, and locks it. Too late, she feels St. Christopher's staff pierce her palm. She closes her fist, shoves both hands into her coat pockets, and walks on.

It is the time of day she never could get used to. "The gloaming" they called it, and the fact that it has a name, that others have felt the vacuum too, has always been a comfort. Today is no exception. She feels a taut smile—the perfect time of day to go.

The store is behind her. She makes her way along the narrow sidewalk, one foot in front of the other. Her shoes are the dark tie-ups she bought to walk around the track after William read how exercise was as good for the head as it was for the body. They walked faithfully for a few weeks, until one morning he went to the porta-potty, and she wandered off the track into the surrounding neighborhood. He found her talking to the postman hours later.

At first there is no sound of water as the sidewalk ascends, only the occasional shadow of geese in flight and a strong smell of old fish. The guardrail is thigh-high and flecked with bird muck. She hikes herself up and over it, to the other side onto a collar of concrete. She presses back against the rail. Watching the river coiled beneath her like a rope, she recognizes what she hasn't before. The sound is huge. Roslyn listens, reassured by the water's wail.

Somewhere a horn blasts, becoming louder and louder, closer and closer. Surely it will pass. She hunches her shoulders as if hiding in her coat, but the honking continues. She raises her hands to her ears and when she opens her palms, St.

Christopher flies from her grasp. She watches the statue tumble through the air, then hit the water.

"Roslyn! Roslyn!" From the corner of her eye a figure comes panting toward her—an arm raised and shaking wildly, demanding attention. Roslyn relents, turning her head and confirming Nicky's voice.

"Damn. I knew it. I said to Mark…" Nicky eases over the rail then motions for Roslyn to sit down and scoot over. "I told him you were out of sorts, and for more than the obvious reason."

Roslyn sucks her bottom lip, unable to speak, even if she had a thing to say.

Nicky produces a red bandana, spits on one corner and clears her space of droppings. She settles down on the rail and the two women sit, elbows on knees, looking at the thick, murky water churning beneath them. An empty froth swirls, where seconds before St. Christopher landed face up and reproachful.

Nicky pulls a pack from her pocket and takes out a cigarette. "Would you look at that?" She gestures toward the river and offers the pack to Roslyn. "All that water, making its way home."

Holding up her hand, Roslyn refuses the pack, then snatches it back. "Home?" she asks.

"The ocean, by way of the gulf. But ultimately the water's headed home."

"Guess it does all end up there. Guess it tries to, anyway."

"Flowing forward. Pushing on, regardless." Nicky flicks open a lighter, lights her cigarette, and holds the flame up for Roslyn.

Roslyn shakes her head. "Don't I know."

"About oceans?"

"About pushing on. Regardless." The cigarette pack is wadded in Roslyn's fist. She squeezes tight, and haltingly begins to describe what's happening to her—how her mind is falling back on itself, back to what had come before, way before, with very little room for everyday. Then she sighs and opens her fingers, before admitting to the most baffling moments of all—the stretches when her mind clears and is every bit its usual self. Only, of course, it isn't. "Until today, I thought the only choice I had was pushing on."

Nicky drags on the cigarette and cranes her neck upward to exhale. "Yep, that's what we do, alright. Push on. Regardless."

The sky is evening bright. Roslyn has worked a cigarette from the pack and now holds it up to Nicky. The lighter's flame wobbles with the hint of breeze, but Roslyn catches it with a fierce inhale.

It is full-on dark by the time Roslyn, claiming to be fine, manages to escape Nicky's protection. Reassured the guardrail's height would not deter her, Roslyn returns to the Pontiac and backs out of the parking lot, only to slam on the brakes and slap her hand against the empty dash. Something's wrong. She switches on the overhead light. There. Her fingers rub the telltale oval stain. She is breathing hard, as if she's done an extra lap around the track. She looks down at her shoes. Is that where she's headed? The track? But surely not in the dark. Her fingers rub the dash. William will know what's missing. William. What was it someone said? Something about everybody going home. That's it. That's where she's going. Home. She leans back against the seat and stares out at the market, lit now with artificial light that hurts her eyes. She squints and is reminded of earlier today. The red front door at Colors. She turns her head back and forth and purses her lips in the mirror. Ha! I'm not going home. I'm going to the hospital. Going to see William.

William's waiting. And won't he be happy? I've remembered!

After a few slow seconds, she presses the power windows wide open, shifts into drive, and nudges the car forward. By the time she's traveled up the small incline and over the bridge, her hair, caught up in the car's momentum, is every bit as tangled as before.

No More Doing Harold

Harold James III drove all the way up to the fourth level of the mall's parking garage because he liked the way his Porsche took the curves, and besides, there weren't many cars up here, so less chance of some fool dinging this baby's paint job. He might as well park at an angle, take up three spaces instead of one, just as a precautionary measure. There was that ratty Ford that had followed him since the second level, but it drove past and took the exit ramp, leaving just a trail of god-awful music in its wake.

Harold turned off the ignition, felt his back pocket for his billfold, and looked down at his shoes, the newest Jordans. Probably too much for mall walking. But a man has to take his plight in life and make the most of it. Fifty-four, with artificial knees and an ornery heart. Yvonne claimed his running days were over. He supposed it was a wife's duty to suggest he take up golf and ride the carts. He'd considered it. But no. If he couldn't hit the pavement running, he'd hit the largest mall in Santa Fe. He could walk five miles without a sweat.

His goal today was to walk one more loop around, enough to take him by Victoria's Secret three times instead of two. He was thinking this as he heard the familiar pounding music approaching from the ramp. He opened the door, and as he did, the Ford came around the corner. Harold sat with the door ajar, waiting for the car with its insufferable music to pass. It came into view, but interminably slow, so slow Harold had time to notice the graffiti on the hood. A blazing red pitchfork surrounded by undecipherable letters. He swallowed and raised his eyes to catch the glare of the red-haired young woman with purple-stained lips gripping the upholstered steering wheel. And were those baseball bats leaning against the backseat between two somebodies in hooded sweatshirts?

It did occur to Harold that he should slam his door and drive like the proverbial bat out of hell down to the first floor, but shaking his head and laughing at his wimpy self, he dismissed the thought. He climbed out of the car just as the driver of the Ford gunned her engine. Harold closed his door. The sooner he got into the organized hum of mall life the better. He raised his keypad and pointed it at the lock.

"Hey man, how goes it?" The Ford had stopped. Music was pouring out of the open doors as three kids got out. They lined up in front of Harold. He turned back toward his car, but something stopped him. Something brought him to his artificial knees. A heavy blow and then another. He pitched forward, letting go of his keys, reaching out to catch the concrete, but his hands felt the weight of someone's boots and his forehead slammed the pavement as the girl—her voice so sweet, so rich with joy—announced she had his keys. His motherfucking keys, and, look, his billfold, and those shoes!

Harold peered through swollen eyes as the sweatshirts untied his carefully double-knotted Nikes, tugged them off his feet, and tossed them into his beautiful machine before climbing in. The scene was fuzzy like a TV on the blink. Yet he knew it was the girl who remained, standing beside him, her dainty hands clutching the bat, and then swinging it above her head. He half-way moaned. He wished he could move his fingers. He wished he could snap them, for here it was—his end. Just like that.

Pending

William is standing in front of the medicine cabinet, his face ripe with whiskered patches. It has been six weeks since he killed his wife and he must move along. Hollow pupils vanish as he swings the mirrored door and scans the shelves of old prescriptions. His fingers tap the sink. The beat is off.

Sanibel, the cottage. He prods himself with what's to come. Their house is on the brink of sold. He reaches down, lifts Roslyn's plastic waste can to the sink, then starts in on this final chore.

Her prescription vials are scribbled on with William's notes: blood pressure WITH MEALS, allergy BEFORE BED, Xanax NO ALCOHOL. He fondles each. The thought, a drop in the bucket, darts from some ironic place inside his head, but he is out of smiles. Her eye mask and earplugs are the last to go. Most items thud on the bottom of the basket, though the eye mask and the earplugs settle quiet as the days have all become.

Except it isn't quiet. From down below, outside on the porch door, a banging persists. William rubs his chin, listening. People don't drop by; there is no use. He refuses their consolation casseroles and pies. Refuses to talk. The "Yo! William!" comes to him now. He feels his face flush, his jaw tighten at the familiar greeting. He sets the waste can on the floor, then gives it a hard kick. One last test, he reckons.

He heads down the hall to the top of the stairs. The floors creak under his bare feet, complaining, as if the house has readied itself for time alone. He goes down the stairs, his left foot waiting for his right. At the landing he stops at the window and rests his forehead on the pane. Outside, the sun is weak but not yet gone. He half expects to see the law. Through limp light, his eyes scan the front hedgerow, branches raucous and unkempt, the PENDING sign rising like a mutant weed.

He tells himself he's almost made it. He hears the back door give.

"You in here, Will?"

He continues his descent, reaching the bottom step just as church bells mark the hour. Around him, the aura of rosewater suggests Roslyn may just have traveled through, on her way to garden club or bridge.

"Hey, guy, you okay?"

William enters the kitchen and faces a long-necked man, younger, with curly red hair, which today is combed and slicked behind his ears. For some time now, ever since William's heart episode, Rhino the handyman has been a fixture in the Meyers's household. Dressed in Carhartt overalls and carrying a six-pack of imported beer, Rhino gives William's shoulder a sympathetic squeeze. "Thought you'd be needing a little refreshment," he says.

William shrugs off the intrusive hand. "Can't say I'm particularly thirsty."

"From the looks of you, I'd say some sort of intervention's in order."

The looks of him. William's belted khaki pants and laundered shirts have gone the way of morning shaves and flossing.

He hooks his thumb over the waistband of his gray sweatpants. Without glancing down at the undershirt he's worn for days, William senses its mix of coffee stains and hand-wiped smudges. Suntanned, broad-shouldered, flat-bellied Rhino is resplendent—even in Carhartts. William grips the linoleum with his bare toes.

Rhino moves to the counter, sets down two beer bottles, then pulls open the refrigerator door. "Geez. Don't remember this baby ever being so empty."

"Yeah, Roslyn kept it stocked."

Her name brings both men to a standstill. William blinks. The light escaping from the open fridge feels garish.

"I remember. Tuna salad. Roast beef. Deviled eggs," Rhino says.

"But," William says, "more and more toward the end, the unexpected. Her purse, car keys, a box of tissue next to the milk."

Rhino shuts the door. "Damn, the fridge isn't all that's empty." He gestures toward the center of the room, where the furniture used to be. "Where'd it all go?"

"Auctioned it all off." William takes two thrift-shop mugs from the cabinet.

"The Queen Anne chair? The pine desk? The sofas?" Rhino's bewildered expression is almost pitiful.

"Ruth took her mother's chair and my army paraphernalia—oh, and the family tree. She took that too. The rest, shoot, too many burdens." William balances mugs and beer. "Nope, an auction was the only way to go. Cleared it all out—everything but our bed. And what's here."

"Sure. Sure. I gotcha." Rhino nods in solidarity.

William uses his foot to nudge a ladder-back chair away from the round kitchen table, the lazy Susan of which holds an array of magazines and photo albums. He sits down and motions for Rhino to join him. "She insisted we buy this ridiculous piece of furniture. Way back all those years ago." He massages a small corner of dull wood, then takes a bottle opener from his shirt pocket. "But then, I guess you know that."

"Roslyn may have mentioned it." Rhino sits. "Everything else—gone? She loved that stuff."

"Some of it, but these last couple of years what she really loved was prowling garage sales and consignment shops, then lugging junk home for you to fix up."

"It made her happy."

"You know, I gotta tell you, the first couple of days after her passing, I sort of veered off course. Wandered around this place like a tourist, trekking through rooms chockful with stuff I never liked."

"She had some doozies."

"She had seven footstools. Always preferred the plaid, squatty one, but she had six others. Preferred the platform rocker when she wrote letters and that monstrous purple chaise when she read."

"Magenta chaise," Rhino says.

"Course she had several other rockers and divans to choose from, just wasn't much interested," William says.

"You think?" Rhino opens his beer.

"What she really liked was seeing your face when she presented you with some broken-down chair, or a scratched-up desk, or a dresser with its innards gone."

Rhino nods. "Or your face, when you saw what I could do with it."

William watches Rhino tilt his mug. "You know, son, before you came into our lives, Roslyn would ream me out for not changing the furnace filters, or caulking around the tub, or taking out the garbage. You know, husbandly chores."

"The worst kind."

"Never seemed to bother you. Mundane chores and working wonders on a piece of junk. How could I compete?"

Rhino opens William's beer. "You were always her prize."

"A damaged one—not good for anything much after my heart scare. A real good for nothing."

"I just tried to take up the slack is all." Rhino stuffs a thick curl behind his ear.

William pushes his mug aside. "Can't help thinking how she'd go on and on about your talent for fixing things like new. Working with your hands. Gifted hands, she'd say." He grips the bottle and takes a swig.

Rhino gives a one-note laugh. "It was good work," he says, using his elbow to swipe a splash of beer off the table.

"Work you could put your heart into?" William asks.

Rhino gulps his beer. "Guess all this explains the sign?"

"Pending? Yessir, the house may be pending, but me, I'm headed down to Sanibel."

"Awfully soon, don't you think?" Rhino asks.

"Not soon enough, Roslyn would say." William rubs his temples.

Many a night after their Billy's accident, he would find her curled beneath the covers, eye mask and earplugs in place since after the ten o'clock news. He'd undress by moonlight, then collapse next to her with a deep breath. They'd lie coiled, her back against his heart.

"What we need is a good dose of Sanibel," she'd offer. He never responded. It wasn't a question, after all.

Rhino burps. "Anyways, grief is tricky. Might want to let

it run its course before you go taking off to a place you haven't seen in years."

Years indeed. William's heart bumps hard against his chest. He downs his beer and returns to the kitchen. "Sage advice coming from one who's never traveled," he says, setting the four remaining beers on the floor between them.

"Roslyn tell you that?" Rhino lifts his brow.

"She may have mentioned it. Obviously she told you about Sanibel."

When Rhino doesn't answer, William reaches across the table and begins to riffle through the stacks of photo albums. "Ah!" he cries. "Look here. Found this tucked among her petticoats and pajamas." He uses both hands to tug a thin leather album from the pile and place it gently on the table in front of them.

Rhino leans back against his chair. The album is covered in a glut of Sanibel stickers. William opens to a page pasted with a forty-year-old article from *Reader's Digest*: "Sanibel—the getaway island of a lifetime."

"For years Roslyn insisted on the honeymoon we kept postponing. I'd landed the manager's position. Couldn't really afford to leave the office just then, but her folks came in from Memphis, kept the babies, and off we went."

"Once." Rhino shifts in his seat.

William turns to send him a quick glare. "Meant to take her back."

"Promised."

"Finish your beer," William says before turning back to the album. "We're biking here, in Egret Alley." They'd pedaled the alley into Egret Village with its labyrinth of white gravel roads, its palm trees, parrots, and tiny cottages on lots the size of porches. An obliging real estate agent had used their camera to take this picture of a younger William grinning at Roslyn, her dark curls bundled in a single yellow bow.

"On a whim we found our way inside a place for sale." William turns the page and clucks his tongue at photos: first of him, hunched and bewildered beneath a ceiling fan, then Roslyn, sitting in a cushioned rocker, beaming.

Rhino lays his finger on the next photo. "That's some bird," he says.

"Some bird." William brushes Rhino's finger away. He remembers how Roslyn cranked open the windows and literally squealed when a great white egret scratched the quiet of their view. As a second bird ascended, Roslyn's gasp was perfect. She whirled away from the window and tugged William close.

"But the real estate agent," he'd said.

"She's gone. It's just us two."

The egrets had begun to mate, the male announcing his intention with a squawk. Roslyn leaned into William. "So harsh," she murmured in his blushing ear, "so undomesticated." She pulled him to the shag carpet. Shell white and mossy soft, it was as far from ordinary as they would ever be.

Afterward, shirts and shorts collected, they moved to the couch, where William retied the ribbon in her hair. "Imagine," Roslyn said, tucking in her blouse, "making do with nothing more than what this place would hold—a life as pure and simple as that." She sat with her back to him, but her remark brought him off the couch.

"A sort of Walden?" He stood in front of her and tried a laugh. "Even that guy, Thoreau, left the pond after a couple of years—built quite a nice home in the city if I recall."

Roslyn jabbed her fingers through her wad of curls. "I

suppose," she said, looking past him. He followed her gaze to find the egrets gone; in their place a pair of common cardinals pecked frantically at rumpled sand.

"And this must be?" Rhino is indicating a freckle-bodied woman lounging in a bathing suit that shows her middle.

William halfway smiles. "We were returning to the motel when Roslyn pulled her bike right up alongside the yard of this gal and asked what it was like living in such a place. 'Well,' the woman said, 'like a fairy-tale—'"

"The happy-ever-after part," Rhino blurts out.

William taps, taps, taps the photo, then makes a fist. "Yeah, that's what she said all right." He looks up from the album. "God, I need a drink. Go bring us the Scotch."

William's gaze follows Rhino to the pantry door. The last of three bottles is in the tin breadbox, on the second shelf, where they stashed it six weeks before.

When Rhino returns with the fifth, William has moved to the foot of the stairs. He gestures for Rhino to follow. With the pat of bare feet and the rub of hard-soled boots, the two men make their way up the stairs. The wastebasket lies where William kicked it, contents scattered on the bathroom floor. When he stops to retrieve a vial that's landed in the hall, a brutal sadness brings him to one knee. He slips the remaining Xanax in his pocket, then, using Rhino's outstretched hand, manages to steady himself and walk ahead.

At the bedroom door, a bracing February draft confronts them. William has left the window open. They enter the room to take their accustomed seats at either end of the four-poster bed, the seats they'd occupied for so many of Roslyn's last hours. They bow their heads, as if giving fate a second chance.

Between them now is the last scene of Roslyn, lying

pillow-propped against the headboard, sipping the cocktail they've prepared. She is wearing the pale-pink nightgown, with the tiny pearl buttons William remembers were tricky to undo. She catches his gaze. "One never knows what to wear to these things," she says before swallowing the fistful of pills he's dropped into her open palm.

Her face softens at the effort of their laughter. William cups her chin in his hand. She is not yet old. She lays her hand on his and reassures him with a laugh as alert and rich as ever.

William is encouraged. "Woman, are you sure about this?"

"It's not too late." Rhino hunches forward.

Roslyn sinks back against the pillows. The faint, sweet smell of her is strong. She sets the empty glass on the bedside table and reaches out for both their hands. "It's all good," she says, her grasp firm even as her breathing slows.

No apologies. No excuses or explanations for why she'd wanted Rhino there. It occurs to William how Alzheimer's freed her from all that and he is glad.

Now, all these weeks later, the chenille spread shimmers in the almost-dark, and her pillows wait, vigilant and fluffed.

Rhino uses the back of his hand to blot tears from his cheek, then opens the Scotch and drinks from the bottle. "To promises kept."

"As opposed to those that weren't?" William accepts the bottle and drinks.

"Her mind took a wallop, but Roslyn never forgot Sanibel," Rhino says.

William takes a firm hold on Rhino's arm. "She say that?"

"Said she loved you. Loved me. Wanted both of us to help her cross."

Though the room has lost its light, the two men stare,

stone-faced now, at one another. Rhino's jaw tightens, William loosens his grip on his arm. The futility of his actions—purging their house of all things Rhino, escaping to Sanibel—astounds him.

Rhino begins to nod, his chin dropping to his chest, his snores soft and guileless. William takes the fifth from Rhino, then lifts the vial of leftover pills from his own pocket. He studies the note scrawled across the bottle's label. FOR THE EVER AFTER.

The happy-ever-after part. Roslyn had mounted her bike. From over her shoulder, she thanked the freckle-bodied woman and sped off. "Wait up!" he had called out, but when he finally reached her, she didn't stop. They careened down sidewalks flanked by bougainvillea and boardwalk bridges over dunes. Following behind Roslyn, his fate inexplicably hinging on the rise and fall of her sandaled foot, William fell into a kind of grace.

Now he uses his thumb to uncap the top of the vial. "Wait up," he says aloud, his voice broken but determined. In the space between dusk and dark, he takes it slow. Two pills to every gulp of whiskey. Across the room, a curtainless window reveals a large white something perched in a tree. A cloud, or a moon, or perhaps two egrets blown off course. William puts the bottle to his mouth and finishes it off, then he closes his eyes and waits for the female bird to sing.

He doesn't die, of course, there on the bed, envisioning an easy exit. No, he recovers. Rhino moves to east Tennessee where he opens an antique store and auction venue. William, his heart now misbehaving worse than ever, allows Ruth to corral him into a perfectly nice nursing home where, though no worse than similar establishments of best intentions, the spongy food, the smell of mentholated rub and cinnamon candy, the fish tank with its eerie glare make William's prickly temperament continue to sour.

He dies in his sleep two years later. An unremarkable death except for the window he manages to pry open, and the breadcrumbs scattered on the ledge for god knows why.

Window Seat

Visiting my mother is never as bad as I imagine. Usually, by the time I drive the two miles from my house to hers, park beside the white picket fence and under the American flag, where she's sure to see that I've arrived, whatever else seemed more important melts away.

But today I tighten my grip on the steering wheel and reconsider why I'm here. Guilt? A new resolve? Funerals tend to churn up both; attending my colleague Ruth's father's service certainly did. "I will be a better daughter," I mumble, frowning down at the Civil War Battle of Nashville flyers askew on the seat beside me. A cover graphic of two horses rearing up beside a young soldier confronts me. Dreadful. I jerk open the car door and make my way to the house.

It's fall. The patio is flush with crisp oak leaves and empty wrought-iron chairs. The perennial garden has been mulched and put to bed; only haughty oriental grass stays behind. My presence brings a flutter of commotion at bird feeders and suet logs that grace Mother's view from where I suspect she lies on the couch with a bout of the punies.

I find her propped up and tucked under the afghan. Her soft pepper-gray hair is limp but for the strands she's curled around her still-beautiful face. A novel of some heft is in her lap, and cigarette smoke stains the air.

"Enjoying poor health, I see." I kiss the top of her head; she pecks the air.

Mother is eighty-four years old. With my younger brother escaping to California, I am the one who must remain vigilant. When Daddy died, I warned Mother she wouldn't be able to keep up the house. Built in 1963, a sprawling two-story colonial—its yard replete with vestiges of Mother's gift for growing—it would be too much. I brought brochures describing carefree residential facilities for active seniors, with the added incentive of assisted living when the time comes. Mother planted more flowers, put up more bird feeders, and painted the kitchen. This was her house, on her land, and she would manage.

Mother has managed. In the three years since Daddy died, she has coped with the house, her finances, and her life with characteristic aplomb. But recently she's taken to the couch. She has a routine. Cancel garden club or church study group or lunch with the ladies. Scoot the coffee table closer to the couch, then set the vase of fresh-picked zinnias or store-bought daises beside the portable phone and the remote. Tug on oversized gray sweatpants and birds-in-a-row sweatshirt, fluff the upholstered pillows, unfold the afghan and—right before collapsing—set a novel, an ashtray, and cigarettes at arm's length.

"What are you up to?" she says, pinching off a wilted zinnia. "Anything?"

I sink into the red plaid chair at the end of the couch. This paneled den, with its perked-up early-American décor, floor-to-ceiling windows, and Granny's rose-colored chandelier, was the epicenter of family life for my brother and me. Silver-framed graduation photos of the two of us stare out from their place of honor atop the TV. A snapshot of Becky, Eddie's wife, is tucked haphazardly in the corner of Eddie's frame. Becky is black. Her mahogany-shaded skin and dark eyes stand in contrast to his Irish red hair and pale complexion.

The remaining smattering of photos—most from years ago—suggests the family's eerie decline. Relatives are scarce, nuclear family even scarcer. We are a barren lot, Daddy would say when considering his lack of grandchildren. With a surge of self-pity, I'm reminded that it's only me now. I am reminded of Eddie's absconding, of shared burdens he's managed to escape.

"What you reading?" I ask.

"Just a silly thriller. I swear, Jamie, I read them and then forget what I've read. Sometimes I'm halfway through before I realize I've read it before."

She doesn't mention the short story collections or the literary novels I've left in the last months. Regardless, I laugh with her, biding my time, waiting to bring up today's agenda. Until now, even though I live close by, the fact that Mother stayed so busy seemed to justify my visits being sporadic. Dropping by whenever I wasn't playing tennis, hiking, or otherwise enjoying my retirement felt perfectly adequate.

"What do you have there?" She nods toward the flyers rolled in my hand. "More nursing home paraphernalia? I told you—"

"No, Mama, I've got a surprise. Read this, I think you'll like it." My enthusiasm sounds genuine, at least I think so.

I hand her a blue leaflet. She looks skeptical. "The Battle of Nashville Monument? So?"

"So, historian Elizabeth Clarkson is doing a series of lectures. Every Tuesday. At the statue that's right down on Twelfth—"

"I know the statue. Heavens, it's been around almost as long as I have."

"But not in its new location—just a mile from here. Anyway, that's where the lectures will be. Lectures on Nashville women who lived during the Civil War. I'll take you. We'll go together. The two of us. Every Tuesday." Was I whining?

I shove up out of the chair and march toward the kitchen. "You want some iced tea?"

Now that Mother is slowing down, I can no longer ignore my obligation to be more present in her life. But visiting seems inadequate. I've vowed to get her out of the house by finding something we might enjoy doing together. This is no small feat. I may be the firstborn, but I am not the first favored. I've never felt particularly close to Mother. Daddy traveled while I was growing up, and Mother had her hands full with Eddie's rambunctious ways. Besides books, it feels like Mother and I have very little in common. No one's fault, really. It's just the way these things unfold.

Iced tea in hand, I breathe deeply, relieved at Mother's lack of enthusiasm. Maybe my antidote to lethargy wasn't such a good idea. Civil War women? Even though I've always felt a sort of kinship with rebellious females, I certainly had no real interest in the Civil War.

But it's too late.

"Tuesdays?" she asks. "Bring me my calendar."

She decides we'll go, even suggesting I might like to read up a bit. "I have a few books in the study someplace," she says.

I gulp my tea. "Thanks, Mama. But honestly, listening to talk of war is one thing; reading about it is overkill."

"You think?" She watches me collect my purse and keys.

I open the back door. "I think," I say and blow her a kiss.

For the next two months, regardless of how she feels the rest of the week, when I arrive on Tuesday, Mother is waiting at the back door, pocketbook in hand, wearing sweater, slacks, and sturdy leather loafers newly polished. We drive a short distance to the corner of Lealand and Battery Lane to meet up with a dozen others in front of the iconic Battle of Nashville Monument. Admittedly, at close range the recently refurbished monument is a sight to behold.

Elizabeth Clarkson is a committed storyteller. Each week she sashays down the hill dressed in the Victorian attire of women such as Adelicia Acklen, Antoinette Polk, or Granny White. "Good stories," she assures us, "can often tell the truth better than nonfiction."

Mother introduces herself to Elizabeth early on and never misses an opportunity to share bits and pieces of her own storied past.

"Your taffeta is luscious," Mother says, touching Elizabeth's splendid gold hoop skirt. Before Elizabeth can reply, Mother tells her how she wore hoop skirts herself as a docent at Belle Meade Plantation in the 1980s. "Don't you just hate the corset?" Mother whispers.

Elizabeth smiles. "Corset? Why no, I don't need a corset; my waist is fine as it is."

Mother's eyes widen. "Oh no, my waist was every bit as perfect as yours, only we were required to wear corsets—to be authentic."

Elizabeth loses her smile. "Interesting," she says, before turning to someone else vying for her attention.

Mother's shoulders slump. "Hey, Mama," I offer, "that's really cool. I didn't know you wore a corset."

She pushes her gold-framed glasses tight. "A corset and

crinolines," she says in the voice I've come to think of as instructive. I nod.

Another time, she tells Elizabeth the story of her great-grandfather's home built near the Punkin Valley railroad depot in east Tennessee. During the war it was occupied by both Union and Confederate soldiers. "When the Confederates were there," Mother's eyes light up, "a baby was born and they called him Tennie. Then, when an Ohio regiment moved in, another baby was born and they named her Ohio—Parlor Ohio, because she was born in the parlor."

"Yes, Tennie and Ohio were rather common names back then," Elizabeth says.

At Elizabeth's tepid response, I speak up. "I love that story, Mama. I'd forgotten about that house in Punkin Valley."

"Still stands, as far as I know."

Whatever slight she may have felt, or I imagined, is quickly forgotten. My mother is good at moving past the unpleasant.

The weeks progress. Elizabeth's lectures focus on the personalities and private struggles of women protecting their homes, land, and families. I think of Mother's refusal to leave her own home. She, too, in her own way, has to fight to keep her land. Only where Elizabeth Harding or Mary Bradford stood firm against the Yanks, Mother stands firm against her only daughter.

I am mildly amused at how fast each hour passes. I've lived in Nashville all my life. Eddie and I tramped around as kids, exploring the hills, creeks, and valleys of many of the same neighborhoods Elizabeth refers to, only now her lively narrative transforms familiar mansions into true homes, common streets into raging battle lines, and neighborhoods into body-blanketed fields of blood and gore.

A culminating field trip marks the final Tuesday lecture. I agree to spend a full day traipsing around Nashville in a toaster-shaped bus full of Civil War fanatics or aficionados, depending on your perspective. We embark at 8:30 on a cold, soupy December morning. I'm wearing a peacoat and jeans; Mother is resplendent in a white wool jacket and dark slacks. We both wear leather gloves but no hat.

Mother, promising to swap later, commandeers the window seat. I settle in beside her as the bus takes off through persistent fog and drizzle. Elizabeth claims she's ordered up just such a day so we will have the true feel for weather conditions during the Battle of Nashville in December 1864. Cold, wet, and foggy.

The bus lumbers down Granny White Pike, passing Sevier Park, which now houses Nashville's Historical Commission.

"Mama, remember the pool?" I hadn't thought of the swimming pool in this park for years.

She squints at the passing landscape as if the pool might appear. "You and Eddie learned to swim there," she says. "It was my summer mainstay until those black families tried to swim and the city closed it."

"And filled it in with dirt," I add. "Planted grass."

"Such a shame," Mother says. I'd like to think she regrets the city's racist attitude, but knowing how it took her years to accept Eddie's marriage, I can't be sure. And I don't ask.

Our family's had its share of drama, and "don't ask, don't tell" is a common response. It is a strategy I resent but rarely challenge. I stare out the window at a revitalized Twelfth Avenue South with shops newly built to look old, or old shops with new facades. Though she and Eddie chose to move where things were just easier for them, Becky has become one of the family, the initial strain of resentment buried and planted over with holidays, birthday gifts, and an occasional hug. It occurs to me that revitalizing family lore might be what helps us to survive, or in some instances to thrive.

Hours later, things are beginning to run together. Generals and their battles, plantations and their slaves. Massacres and mayhem ad infinitum. I need a nap, but we are beginning our final stretch toward Franklin Road and Father Ryan High School. Eddie attended Ryan. A wave of missing my brother breaks through me.

Elizabeth stands and begins to read poems penned by Father Ryan during the Civil War.

"O'er the hills the twilight, in the vale 'tis dim. And life's fitful mystery steals into a hymn."

Eddie, as mother tells the story, lives a life larger than our Southern town can swallow. I know Mother pines for his return, but she never complains and certainly never cries. In fact, I've never seen my mother cry. I reach over and squeeze her sturdy, sun-worn hand. I'm surprised when she doesn't flinch. I tighten my grip.

The bus approaches the end of the tour, and I'm feeling a bit let down. Beside me, Mother's face is closed and distant. Have I been expecting some grand coming together? Where is the music, the final crescendo, proclaiming all is well between us?

By the time I drop Mother off and arrive home, there's an email from Elizabeth announcing her next event. *The Life and*

94

Times of Nathan Bedford Forrest Bus Tour—Battles, Skirmishes, and Historic Sites. Staring at the computer screen, finger poised atop delete, I recall how once, after I'd done some unremarkable favor for her, Mother accused me of wanting to ingratiate myself.

Cautiously, my gaze shifts. From the leafless, gnarly oak outside my window, one lone bird feeder, a retirement gift from Mother, dangles empty and unused. I think of how she delights in watching cardinals, bluebirds, and jays visit her profusion of feeders. Mine is tube-shaped, which, Mother assured me, any bird can land on and eat, regardless of body size.

It occurs to me how, in this story—the one I choose to tell—Mother intended to present me with a bit of the view she herself has come to love. I feel a smile coming on as I reread Elizabeth's description of the next bus tour, then hit print. Mother will want to go, of course. It's on a Tuesday.

What It Takes

From the vantage point of years—a decade's worth—I imagine Marlene fanning the plump dark fingers of her hand across the textbook pages, studying the lightning bolts tattooed on her thumbs. Her nails are the color of the storm. A shout of thunder turns her head, but a window shade hides the view. She ducks, thinking next time she will ask for stars.

The child is slumped across an open book, her chin snug against the War of 1812. "Marlene, get your things," Mrs. Merrick, the principal, says. I feel the girl cringe but see her do what she is told. As a professor of teacher education—a teacher of teachers—I have spent the last decade avoiding schools, and now I remember why. Being in a school can break your heart.

The girl sits up, and the other sixth graders suddenly seem small. She jams the history book, then the paper wads and notebooks sprouting from beneath her desk, into a purple backpack water-stained a rusty blue. The class is watching; she smiles, close-mouthed, to no one but herself.

In the hall, Marlene and I follow Mrs. Merrick and yellow Greeley tiger paws to two metal desks. Mrs. Merrick motions toward the desks while making introductions. "Now Dr. Meyers, I'll just let you and Marlene get acquainted." She pats my shoulder before rushing down the hall, leaving a faint sigh in her wake.

I fit myself into the desk like Alice in that land of hers. I am reluctant to begin, silenced by all I know about myself: my contradictory self, my posing self. I've offered to tutor here at Greeley Middle School, not out of benevolent goodwill, but simply to meet the university's new community service mandate.

"Sorry to pull you out of class," I say.

The girl bends her head and mumbles, "That's okay," before raising her eyes, "but it was my favorite class."

"History is your favorite class?"

"Yes ma'am."

"What are you studying?"

Marlene makes a circular motion with her right foot. She wears black high-topped basketball shoes; there is a bracelet of dark skin beneath her jeans, where socks should be. Her foot stops on its third rotation. She stares across the empty hall and clutches the front of her desk with both hands.

"You know Waterloo?" she asks.

"Napoleon's Waterloo?"

She shrugs. "My brother. He knows—we're doing a report."

"He's helping?" I am leaning forward now, craning to catch her glance.

"He's smart. He goes to State—his name is Thurman."

"I teach at State."

She turns, giving me a glimpse of her top tooth: shiny white but jutting beaver-like from its upper gum. Marlene speaks from behind an open palm. "He's going to graduate and get us a car," she says. "He works Burger King and stuff, so it's taking him a long time."

Her candor disarms me. She's probably used to being poked

and prodded with concern from school personnel, and I suspect she's learned her lines. When I fail to respond, she persists. "He's teaching me to dance," she says, and her cheeks rise, lifted by a hidden smile.

I never met her brother. My sense of him is drawn from polished steps to his upstairs room that leaks Puccini, the *Southern Living* and *People* magazines he presented to his mother, and the potted plants he tended on the stoop. Once I arrived at their house just as he was coming out. A small and wiry man, his white shirt starched to perfection, he moved gracefully across the lawn toward the car parked in front of me. Suddenly he stopped, shot a glance through my windshield and saluted. As I opened my car door, he opened his, and by the time I climbed out he was gone.

On my second school visit, we drag our desks into a long narrow storage closet and sit facing each other, desktops touching. The room smells of wilted paper products, discarded textbooks, and moths left to fry in the milky shield of a fluorescent light blinking overhead.

"There, that's better." I stretch my legs and prop my foot on a low shelf of discarded spelling books.

"They did say find a space." Marlene's giggle spurts too large. She pulls a pair of glasses from the pocket of her backpack. Serious glasses, thick-lenses and black. She holds them with both hands, then pushes them on her nose.

"I've brought some paper and pencils. Let's do some writing," I say. There is no real plan here. No one has asked how I will proceed, so I do what I teach my students they must do once they are teachers—learn all they can about their kids, and writing is the best way to get started.

"Can I see the pencils?" she asks.

I hold out three pencils, blue with State University stamped on the side.

"Do the erasers work?"

"They're brand new, I'd imagine they work."

She sits, slack-jawed, as I place pencils and paper on our desks. The word "fragile" comes to mind, Mrs. Merrick's label for a child whose test scores fall erratically between learning disabled and normal, a range that lends itself to mere opinion. "You'll have no trouble with Marlene. A sweet child—in an off kind of way—very well behaved."

"Tell me what you like most about yourself," I say.

"Which parts?"

"Any parts: the way you look, what you do well, your family, or your life." I'd read a report. Evaluators suspect fetal alcohol. Her mother has been known to run drunk through the school screaming obscenities.

"I live in a pink house."

"Okay, let's write that down." Though I haven't seen the house, I suspect she's fibbing about the color. Maybe a sign of coping.

Marlene's print is careful. "Your turn," she says.

"I live in a brick house," writing what I say aloud.

"I fix hair." Marlene writes without my prompt.

"I like to garden," I write, though I don't garden; it is something I can add to keep things moving.

"I am half Indian. My granny was an Indian," Marlene says.

"I am Irish. My great-grandmother came over from Ireland." And she did. We both write.

The bell rings. Marlene stands and holds out her paper.

"Keep the pencil," I say.

Marlene slips it behind her ear. She removes her glasses and stuffs them in the pocket before she walks out the door, then vanishes into a hall alive with kids. Her rapid departure confounds me. I am disappointed. I want the girl to acknowledge the hour. I want her to say she enjoyed it, or at least ask if I am coming back. I want Marlene to say thank you.

Marlene's teachers are concerned. They watch for signs she's veered off course—her mother, after all, is crazy. They tell me stories, insisting I should know. Their anecdotes pile inside my head like tabloid pages. I find myself envisioning a life beyond my encounters. From all I am told, and what Marlene herself will choose to share, I find a story.

I imagine Marlene stepping into the hall where the thank you she'd been saving couldn't go. The crush of bodies, book bags, and noise carry her around the corner and out of sight of the teacher who writes with her in the closet, Miss Ruth. A hint of happy stirs her insides, making today's walk toward the cafeteria better than other days. She pulls her shoulders back and moves through the throng of kids as if this hall—with its repeated pattern of mascot paws painted on the floor, its stately lockers, its smell of warm skin and cheese pizza—belongs to her as much as them.

As she approaches the double doors, the happy wavers. She hasn't worn her glasses, and, when she enters, a haze of mass confusion looms.

"So, what's up with you missing class?" Brittany from first period stands in Marlene's path. Marlene ducks her head and stifles a giggle. Brittany pokes a finger at her chest. "I'm here to tell you my mom is fed up. I'm warning your fat ass. She's calling your house to tell your folks how you all the time calling everybody. All the time with that crazy person laugh. My mom says you is har-ras-ing us." This last is accompanied by three sharp jabs.

Marlene will not buckle. She juts out her chin and takes a deep breath, producing a chest this Brittany might well envy. Without a word, Marlene flicks around and blows through doors just entered. Even without her glasses she is able to follow the repeated tiger paws underfoot and can easily imagine the surge of kids who move away to let her pass, their faces struck with awe at how courageously she carries herself. The thought is enough to bring tears to her eyes.

I do come back. Twice a week for an hour each visit. We have a routine, the same routine I often tell my students they should try. The first ten minutes of the session, I read picture books by Lucille Clifton, or chapter books by Lois Lowry, or poems by Shel Silverstein. Next, we write. Timed writings, I explain, involve writing anything that comes to mind for ten minutes without stopping. Anything. Even if you only write your name, you can't stop. I bring more pencils, along with pens and lots of paper: lined and unlined, fancy stationary and postcards, legal pads and spiral notebooks. Marlene helps herself, and then we write.

September 20. Marlene Marlene Marlene Brooks MARLENE BUFORD BROOKS Marlene Buford Brooks MARLENE

BUFORD BROOKS MMB mmb MARLENE BUFORD
BROOKS Marlene Buford Brooks …

September 20. Sitting in a storage closet at Greeley Middle
School. Marlene seems to have a lot of friends. She speaks of
Ginny, Tomika, Brittany and others. My friends—she beams—
are coming to my birthday party!

And I imagine Marlene slipping on her glasses to study the
crow's pin-stiff legs and gnat-covered glare. She uses her tennis
shoe to nudge it off the stoop, then takes her place on the top
step, knees hugged tight, and waits. A Chevrolet the color of
wet dirt rumbles to a stop against the curb. The driver lays his
arms against the steering wheel and rests his head against his
arms. Marlene slips her glasses into her shirt pocket, preferring
just the blur of knowing Thurman's home. In the time it takes
for her to decide not to share her day, he climbs out of the car
and strides across the yard.

"Too cool for you to be out here," he snaps.

"Yeah, well, I'm fixin' to go in." She stands and points at the
dead crow. "Had to clean the mess."

"Damn that cat."

"Wisdom."

"Huh?"

"His tag says Wisdom. Want me to call the number on the
tag? I got it." She pulls out a small spiral note pad from her
jeans. "I'll need the phone."

Her brother climbs the three steps to stand beside her. He
smells like new pennies. "No phone. No." It's been a week since

he unplugged their phone and stashed it in his upstairs room. "Give me that." He grabs the pad and flips through the pages. "Just what I thought. Where do you get all these numbers?"

The giggle that escapes her feels retarded. A jagged laugh that hurts inside her head. "My friends. All of them."

"Well, your friends are sick of you, and your constant calling."

She jerks the pad out of his hand and winces as he throws open the screen and pushes through the front door. "Is that my boy?" If only her friends were standing here. She begged them to keep their mothers from calling the house complaining of Marlene's after school calls. If only Ginny and Heather and Tomika and Brittany were on this porch and could hear her mother's feeble "Is that my boy?" they'd understand. Her mother isn't well and must not be disturbed. One wrong move, one look, could whip her off the couch and into a fury of screams so hard you'd scramble underneath your bed and press your ears.

October 1. Marlene hands me her work for safekeeping. I've promised not to look, and, so far, I haven't. It goes in a rose-covered folder I've had stashed in my desk for ages—maybe since I student-taught.

"So why me?" she asks.
"Why not you?"
"How'd you figure me a writer?"
"Just lucky I guess."
"You too?"
"Lucky?"

"I was Granny Thelma's lucky charm."

"I wouldn't say I was lucky, but maybe your charm will work for me as well."

"Ha!"

She draws a picture: me in my brown suit, cinched and scarfed; me in high-heel shoes and on my pixie-puffed brown hair I wear a crown of four-leaf clovers. Giggling, she adds a title. LUCKY LADY RUTH's mouth is gaping open and her eyes are closed.

The first time we eat lunch together, I am late. I fill my tray with fish sticks, applesauce, and banana pudding, then stand aside until I see Marlene. The girl walks with the halting gait of one whose eyesight has gone bad, or, as I've figured out, one too proud to wear her ugly glasses. I make my way across the room, watching as Marlene finds a table, empty at one end. I walk faster, but by the time I arrive the boys at the other end have started taunting.

"Hey fang, it's daylight, shouldn't you be underground?"

I slide onto the bench across from Marlene. "Sorry, kid," I say. "The day got away from me."

Marlene hesitates, and then gives a loud whoop before pulling her lunch out of her backpack. Squinting, she uses both hands to unfold the greasy Burger King bag.

"Hey girl, get OUTTA here with that stinky shit." One boy slams his hand down on the table.

I glare in his direction. Marlene doesn't flinch; she takes out a cold hamburger and a napkin full of fries.

"You get that from the trash?" a different boy joins in.

I stare harder, then look at Marlene and understand she

doesn't want my help. She rips open three salt packets and emp-ties them onto her meal. "That's okay, Miss Ruth. Ha! Some days are just hard to catch."

…she had a report due to me…it was to be on explorers…she turned in one on Jimmy Carter…go figure…I confronted her, she just rolled her eyes. I know people do that as a defense…they don't realize how irritating it is.

"What is it they're telling me about your work?" I ask, un-locking the storage room and waving her in. Our desks are waiting.

"I'm not doing it. Haven't put my mind to it."

She sits down and puts her glasses onto the desk. Her stare feels blurred.

"Why not?"

"I'm doing a report on Columbus."

My mind scurries to follow her logic. "Why is your assign-ment late?"

"I did the wrong thing. I did it on Carter."

"What did you learn about Carter?"

"He has a wife named Rosalynn. He was president a long time ago."

"Where did he live?"

"Somewhere in Virginia?"

"I thought it was Georgia."

She slides her glasses on and takes a pencil from my desk. "No," she says, sitting tall, "I know it wasn't Georgia." Her smile might be a snarl if you didn't see how well it hid her wayward tooth.

I intend to suggest she check her facts, but something in the way she's braced herself stops me. We read instead.

I've brought *Cousins* by Virginia Hamilton. Marlene and I

read alternate pages of chapter one aloud. Her voice is clear and expressive as she reads about Cammy visiting her Gram in the nursing home and how the grandmother begs Cammy not to leave because they have work to do on nonexistent curtains.

I read the line "she closed her heart down" and ask Marlene what it means to close your heart. She shrugs, and I start in about how when someone you love is hurting and you want to make it better but there is nothing you can do, you close down your heart and go on as best you can.

"That's exactly how I felt when I left my father in the nursing home." I am teary-eyed, remembering Daddy's recent funeral, remembering how, after losing my brother in a wreck and Mom to Alzheimer's, he finally lost his will to live. "You're probably too young to know…"

"I know," she says, and reaches across our desks to pat my hand.

November 7. Marlene Buford Brooks MARLENE BUFORD BROOKS Marlene Buford Brooks MARLENE BUFORD BROOKS … what to write what to write anything my name my I am a walker I am a slow walker I am slow we leeve last after the bus and car riders I wear my glasss when I walk across the yard past Mrs. Johnson at the croswalk and on to home I am Marlene Buford Brooks…

I can see the puffy coat Marlene has pilfered from the lost and found; it grows warm as she sits at her desk and waits for car and bus riders to leave. When the PA calls for walkers, she shuffles down the hall, out the big glass doors, and down the steps. The cold frame of her glasses is heavy on her nose, but she sees fine, walking over dirt-packed lawn, standing by the curb, and waiting for Ms. Johnson's signal.

Once across the street, Marlene walks fast, but her mind is faster: she is drinking V-8 on the couch in her house down the corner from the church, having crossed the tracks after walking down two streets of houses holding porches with no men.

"Girl, where's you goin' in such a hurry? Come on now, how was school?" The gravelly voice pulls her mind back to where she is—walking quickly down the street, tracks still up ahead. She sharpens her gaze, focusing on the signal post and its winding stripe of red as she keeps moving. The voice calls after her with foolishness her brother warned her to ignore, and though she keeps walking, seeing just the twisting stripe of red—new paint red—she feels the old man's stare and knows his longing like she knows her own. It is the kind that stretches your insides with its hope and closes your heart with its awful fear. These thoughts carry her to the tracks where she clasps the post for luck, then pushes her glasses firmly on her nose and leaps across.

At times, the wanting and the real get all mixed up, and she says stuff that leaves her wishing she had just shut up. She slips her hands under crossed arms and walks with her chin tucked against her chest. Her birthday party is tomorrow after school, and she has invited Brittany, Ginny, Tomika, and Heather—all her friends. Miss Ruth is coming too. Marlene reaches the main thoroughfare and lets its sidewalk carry her past the cleaners where Thurman played the numbers, and the market where her mother bought the beer. There'll be eleven candles on her cake…vanilla is her favorite, with chocolate frosting… M-A-R-L-E-N-E will be in blue.

She stops at the church. The message on the marquee invites all to "find your faith and your doubts will starve." Miss Ruth would like that. It makes a person think, and Miss Ruth was always asking her to think. Or telling her she had. Good thinking, she said. Marlene turns on Georgia Street. Her street. Tucked deep inside a raggedy little neighborhood, this street is a treasure. She feels the bump of pride she always feels as she climbs the hill. She hopes Miss Ruth will notice how the street rises, how down there is the mess you left behind, but up here you are with the quiet houses.

November 8. I tell my students not to get attached. Kids have families and friends, what they need are teachers. So be a teacher—not a mom or dad or friend—Ruth Meyers, Dr. Ruth Meyers, Dr. Meyers...

A block from public housing, the yards surprise me. Neat patches of grass, with shrubs sheared and shaped like trees. And—look at that—a view! I steer with one hand while I re-check Marlene's directions. 1607 Georgia, up the street from Hadley Church. No mistake. I park on the curb. The house is pink; it sits like a lump of taffy on the tongue of a sloping lawn. My fingers tighten around the steering wheel. Like roots, they curl and clutch, and I watch them, waiting to let go.

On the front porch, I stand between a ficus plant and a t-shirt hung to dry, trying to decide where on the flimsy-framed screen door to knock.

I tap lightly. "Who's there?" Marlene's voice is vibrant.

"It's me. Miss Ruth." There is laughter, and the door opens, though no one appears. Leave. I pull the screen door towards me and step inside.

There are no rugs. The floor is dull but spotless, the air is a mix of cigarette smoke, fried bacon, burnt coffee, and a touch of disinfectant. I see the doll before I see Marlene, though both are on the floor beside crumpled wrapping paper and a K-Mart bag.

"Looks like someone's opening presents," I say.

"It's a Barbie with hair that I can comb and fix without a fuss," Marlene says. I understand the comparison to her own thick hair; "the beast" she calls it—hair she can't comb without a pick. Your hair is as soft as dog hair, she said once, patting my curls.

My gift is wrapped in silver foil and tied with purple ribbon; I hand it to her.

"You have a seat now, Miss Ruth." A woman, sitting on a large-cushioned couch across the room, pats the space beside her. From a hard brown face, her eyes shine.

"Mrs. Brooks?" I approach slowly, as if any sudden movement might upset the woman. "Thank you for inviting me to Marlene's party."

Mrs. Brooks wears cut-off jeans, flip-flops, and a Titans football jersey. She is small and, next to my large frame, seems even smaller.

"No problem, no problem. Make yourself at home." She says, grabs my outstretched hand with both of hers.

Marlene sits cross-legged on the floor. She holds up the unwrapped *Who Is Carrie?* "A book?" she asks.

"A history book. Carrie is a young black girl living during the American Revolution."

For the next hour, I do try to make myself at home. There are no other guests. There is no chocolate icing, but the caramel

cake's Happy Birthday is punctuated with a candy rose, and
the grape cola is tasty. And there is a sort of conversation—
about the weather and the pictures on the wall. An oversized
black-and-white portrait of a woman's face—full of flesh, but
solemn—hangs next to the painting of a Spanish conquistador
dressed for battle. No one knows his name, but hers is Thelma.

I smile. Thelma Lorraine Clark, Marlene's half African, half
Native-American grandmother died a year ago. Granny Thelma
read me stories, the girl said; she also confessed that the portrait, floating life-like in the dark, sometimes made it hard for
her to sleep.

"You know, there is an African-Indian museum in Florida,"
I say, before drinking the last of my soda. I wipe the bottom
of my cup with my hand and set it on the coffee table beside a
People magazine.

"Why, that's just fine. Babe, you hear that? A museum in
Florida," Mrs. Brooks says, slipping off her flip-flops and drawing her legs beneath her on the couch.

Is this the mother they warned me about? I try to imagine
her running through the school howling obscenities, or spend-
ing time in jail for using drugs. I take a small breath.

Marlene collects the plates and stands facing us from the
kitchen door. Today her hair is piled high and laced with dozens of tight brown braids that fall around her throat like jewels.
She doesn't speak; there is something regal about her.

I stand up, but as I begin to walk in her direction, she moves
to block the view, and I pretend not to see the cockroaches
crawling up the kitchen wall, slithering over the stove. I lay my
arm across Marlene's shoulder and pull the girl towards the
front door.

"Happy birthday, kid," I say, hugging her quickly, but with

both arms. Marlene keeps her own arms by her sides and smiles her tight-lipped smile as I make my quick good-byes, then step outside. In the car, I roll down the window enough to find fresh air. The something antiseptic I smelled inside? Bug spray, I realize now.

When Mrs. Brooks's face appears, filling up the half-opened window, I cry out. She shoves a photograph at me. "Here she is at five. Take it with you," she says.

I take the snapshot, still startled. "Thank you, Mrs. Brooks, but..." I do not want her creased and faded keepsake. Too late. She has turned and is skittering, bird-like, down the slope, back across the yard.

I drive along the street and stop at the church before looking closely at the picture of little girl Marlene: her brown eyes free of thick-lensed glasses, her mouth without its wayward tooth. The camera captured her smile at its onset, before she might have reined it in. I turn the picture over and read the back:

To Granny from her lucky charm

Marlene Buford Brooks Age 5

The handwriting is surely that of a Marlene older than five. Each word seems painfully correct, printed in minuscule letters that float proud and unrepentant against the page.

In the eight weeks we've spent together, I managed to keep things in their proper place. Teacher. Student. Nothing more. I place the photograph face up on the seat beside me, start the car, and drive on. The nothing more is for a reason, but by the time I arrive home, I can't, for the life of me, remember what it is.

I've lived in the same five-mile radius my entire life. Green Hills, a bedroom community of Nashville, oozes middle-class respectability. There's a kind of subtle preeminence in the idea of Green Hills as a safe, politically correct kind of place compared to the neighboring old money elitism of Belle Meade or new money tackiness of Brentwood. Green Hills emits an air of conscious living.

Still, my friends weren't being facetious twenty years ago when I told them I'd be teaching at State and they asked if I'd be safe. What they knew about this predominately black land grant college "on the other side of town" was drawn from frequent newspaper reports of crimes occurring on the edge of State's north Nashville campus.

Many things have changed since I found my way those mere six miles from Green Hills to the Clay Hall College of Education. Under a court order to recruit more whites, millions of dollars were allocated to spruce up the campus and, after a while, the shades of student faces grew more diverse.

What hasn't changed so much is news of drug arrests, domestic violence, and an occasional murder in the neighborhood just outside our reach—where the money stops and poverty, like an old sore, is hard to hide.

I drive like an alert tourist, mindful of my door locks, the three blocks from campus to 1607 Georgia Street. My route takes me past the clash of marigolds and zinnias spilling over porches lined with vinyl chairs and green metallic gliders, past sharp-shouldered women dodging men on bicycles, past boys on bus benches, and dogs who sniff the sidewalk cracks for crumbs.

I never lose the fear of Marlene's neighborhood or the dread of roaches, and, after a while, I visit only long enough to figure out a reason for us to leave. Marlene does not like crowds. What she likes is riding in my Civic, turning on the radio and pushing the button we set to Nashville's Voice-of-Soul. She likes drive-through restaurant chili dogs and soft-serve ice cream in a cup. She likes the park if we can find a table without people; otherwise, she'd rather stop and roll the windows down and watch. Sometimes Marlene brings a fistful of dollar bills—which I wonder about, but never ask. Can we go to the Dollar Store and buy a shirt, to Pic-n-Pay for shoes? Leary of cheap clothes that will not last, I drive to Dillard's. Marlene keeps her money; I will pay.

It is spring break, and I am having lunch with Jamie, a recently retired colleague.

"How are you adjusting to life as an orphan?" Jamie has attended both my parents' funerals. I chuckle at her gentle tease.

"How're things with your mom?" I ask. Jamie's role as caretaker to her widowed mom is an ever-present concern.

She shrugs. "Mom is mom and I'm managing to keep above the fray."

"Wish I could say the same—I seem to be sliding more and more into the fray." I laugh, then proceed to fill her in on my community service.

"Sixth grade, god what an awful year," she says.

"I'd forgotten how ugly schools can be—and chaotic. The hardest part is getting settled in, reminding Marlene what we plan to do each week. I'm never sure what she remembers. It's like her week of living has wiped away our time the week before."

"But you like the girl?"

"She interests me. She has this haughty way about her—to tell you the truth, the child has captivated me." I try not to gush about feeling useful—feeling real. A long time ago, Jamie accused me of being like a moth flying to the light of hopeless causes; with my increasing preference for safe routine, there's been no need.

"Is that wise?" Eyes lowered, Jamie leans back against the cushioned booth and unfurls her napkin. "As my mother likes to say, there's a fine line between helping and rescuing."

"Ha!" I say and recognize I'm echoing Marlene's signal for sudden insight. "Maybe advocate is what I am."

Jamie sips her wine. "That's a loaded word."

I venture further. "I've actually been thinking I'll see what I can do about her glasses—and her tooth. Surely there's a way..."

"Careful, Ruth," Jamie says, "take it from one who knows—don't get sucked in."

That afternoon I find myself at Marlene's house. The door has lost its screen, and the ficus tree has moved inside.

"Miss Ruth, Miss Ruth, you come in." Mrs. Brooks squints at the intruding light.

"I was on my way to the library and thought Marlene might like to join me."

"She's walked to the store. Can you wait a bit?" Mrs. Brooks lifts a thin blanket from the couch and wraps it around her shoulders. "I been sick you know. Sick today and sleeping." On the floor beside the couch is a plastic tumbler; the faint smell of beer mingles with the smell of Raid. "You sit down now and we can talk. I been meaning to."

The cushion springs sink beneath me as I sit where Marlene usually does, in the over-stuffed chair facing Granny Thelma's portrait and Thurman's room up the flight of stairs across the hall.

"I get down in the back and have to take to bed," Mrs. Brooks continues. "You know, there was a time, Miss Ruth, when I used to work for some of the finest ladies in this town. You know a Dr. Caldwell, Dr. Duncan Caldwell, lives on that—what is the street? Where the governor lives?"

"Curtiswood?"

"Yeah, that's it. That's the last place I worked. Why, I went there twice a week, sometimes more if there was a party. Miss Katie would say she couldn't get along without her Nel."

"I'm sorry you're sick."

"You know my boy? Thurman?"

"Marlene talks about him so much, I feel as though I do," I say, trying not to sound annoyed that Thurman always manages to be gone when I am here.

"He's the one that keeps us now. Working nights and weekends and going to school. Still, he covers our bills."

"I'd love to meet him. He should stop by my office."

"He should, but Miss Ruth, he don't like your kind."

"The teacher kind?"

"The white kind."

I slide my hands between the cushion and my thighs.

"Not that you'd know it," Mrs. Brooks says. "He's around you folks a lot. One thing he learned while I was working was how to wait tables and pass the liquor tray. He's got himself a second part-time job with a caterer. Wears a uniform and looks important."

I have stopped responding, but the woman doesn't notice.

"The thing is, he's all we got. Lives upstairs and plays his music. He don't complain, but it ain't fair." Mrs. Brooks reaches for the empty tumbler, then lights a cigarette instead. "What I want to say is, you should let Marlene come clean your house."

I watch a flurry of smoke escape from the woman's nostrils.

"Yes, well, I'll keep that in mind," I say, shifting my gaze to the portrait on the wall where thin threads of smoke disguise the set of Thelma's jaw but not her eyes. The photo of Marlene's grandmother meets my gaze with a look that could hold the hope of ages or the treason of an afternoon.

"Hey!" I stand up as Marlene walks in the door.

"Look at her, Miss Ruth—don't she look like she's getting even fatter? Turn around and let Miss Ruth see how tight those jeans are."

"Mama, how you feeling? I brought you a Clark bar and a Dr. Pepper from the store."

"I was just telling Miss Ruth what a fine job you'd do cleaning her house."

"I stopped by to see if you might want to go to the library, but, well…it's getting late. Could we do it another time?" I am talking too fast.

The girl gives me a smile I read as grateful. She hurries across the room to kiss the top of her mother's head before handing her the cola and candy. I move toward the door, then, resisting the impulse to retrieve Marlene, I say good-bye.

By summer, Marlene has a new friend. Herb used to go to school with her but dropped out to get his mouth fixed. I imagine how he describes his upcoming surgery: how each tooth must be pulled, how it will hurt so bad they can only take out two at a time and then he'll have to return for more. It might take months. All of this will start any day so he doesn't figure he should stay in school, which would just be interrupted anyway. Marlene was separating darks from whites on the laundromat floor when this boy she remembered from homeroom nodded across the aisle. By the time he'd come over to tell her about the surgery, she'd tossed the underwear in with the shirts and snapped the washing machine closed. He dropped two quarters in the slot and asked if she would like a root beer.

She likes the way his red hair looks cared for, parted precisely to the left of center, showing pink skin, the edges razor-trimmed to graze his neck when he walks to get the drinks. She remembers how, in fifth grade art class, the smell of beer drew her attention to the door where her mother stood, arms stretched and clinging to the doorframe, her thin body thinner in a cotton sundress and no shoes, her eyes with that trapped mouse bulge, and the gibberish falling from her mouth was very loud. She remembers how Herb had come up afterwards and laughed. "If it makes you feel any better, my mom has been known to throw every pot she owns out our kitchen window onto the sidewalk five flights below—people have been almost killed!" His shrug brought the world back in focus.

He lives a bus transfer away from Georgia Street, so some days he comes by. Marlene fixes him a mayonnaise and peanut butter sandwich, she drinks V-8, and, if her mother's home, they watch TV. Nel's favorite is *The Jerry Springer Show*.

But today, Nel is out. Herb has helped Marlene fix a window screen ripped open by a nigger trying to break in. Herb no longer winces when she says the word, as if he too understands her need to separate herself from those who act the fool. They are sitting on the stoop playing with Wisdom. Herb is dangling a piece of twine between the cat's paws when Marlene snatches the string and jumps up, hiding it behind her back. Herb stands too and, reaching for the string with both hands, finds Marlene wrapped there in his arms. Ha! she warns and laughs a real and sprightly laugh—a laugh he needs to quiet with a kiss.

With the beginning of a new school year, I help Marlene get organized for seventh grade. We practice making lists, allotting time for homework assignments, keeping class notes in different colored folders. For a while, her teachers assure me, it all seems to help. Still, there is no pattern to what Marlene will and will not remember. I tell myself a girl can only live with so much before something gives, and so I try not to impose my need for structure. I try to be flexible, see it from her perspective, until she starts forgetting her glasses. This, I tell her, is unacceptable.

"But I like for you to read to me," she says.

"That is not the point. Not bringing your glasses is a sign of immaturity. It is a sign you just don't care."

She sighs, then unzips her backpack and dumps the contents on the floor. My heart sinks. Crinkled sheets of notebook paper, random folders, half-done worksheets, a history book, a grammar book, a green comb and a brown pick, two balled up paper sacks, and yes, the remnants of her glasses.

I lift both pieces from the pile. She waits—for praise or punishment I'm not sure. I am in a sort of twilight zone, where everything that's come before is nothing I can count on now.

"When did this happen?"

Her face takes on its boast. "Ha!" she cries, returning now to the day a single backslap—an upper classman telling her to move along—severs her glasses. I imagine the force of his large palm on her pack, smacking the only pocket still intact, the one she trusted with her eyes. At first, she doesn't realize what has happened, then I see she does. I see her making her way to the girls' restroom. She slams her bag on top of the radiator and traces her finger over the pocket before reaching in and pulling out first one half, then the other; the nose bridge is sliced clean, but the lenses are still intact. She holds two sides up to the light in front of her eyes.

Ha! No good. Any fool would tell you that—would understand why she went without. Ha! She drops each part of her glasses to the bottom of her pack and hitches it up on her shoulder. I see her stride out the door past a wad of girls just coming in. She is used to blurred edges, now she'll just get used to more.

I ask her if her brother knows. She is agitated by the question. I imagine how she and her mother will wait together for Thurman to come home, each for her own reason. They watch a Cosby rerun and, to pass the time, Marlene fixes Nel's hair. Marlene is good with hair. She can do it with her eyes closed. Nel is stretched out on the couch, reaching down, stirring the ashtray with her finger, looking for a butt that's not quite done.

They don't hear the car, but Thurman's key in the lock brings the room to attention. He steps through the door with the urgency of a passerby. Thurman's skin is the brown of a paper bag. His dark eyes reflect the twinkle of a small gold hoop attached to his left ear. He is dressed in black, except for tennis shoes that, with the dust of an afternoon, have lost their white.

Cliff Huxtable is teaching Denise how to dance. One two three, one two three. He demonstrates over and over, until his daughter gets it. Marlene half hopes for a reprieve, hopes Thurman will not stop, will not have time to listen. An accident, Herb reminded her. Not your fault—now tell him. Marlene turns off the TV.

"My smokes?" Nel reaches up to catch the pack he pulls from a pocket and tosses.

"My Snickers?"

"Kid," Thurman says, narrowing his eyes at Marlene and holding his hands apart, "you getting way too wide in the hide." He is headed toward the stairs, but she moves in front of him. She turns and bends over, shaking her backside and slapping her hands on her hips. "Here you go, brother. Here's what I think!" She begins to laugh, but by the time she stands to jerk around and thrust her face in his, she is screaming. She screams to stop whatever is around her. To give her time to think what she should do. She screams, convinced it is the only way to make it to what happens next.

By the time Thurman grips her face to stuff her cheeks into her mouth like gauze, she's ready. "My glasses," she chokes, "are busted."

Thurman squeezes harder, then pushes her away. She rubs the side of her mouth and touches her tongue to her top lip. Her fang has left its mark. She flops into the chair under Granny.

"I told you, you can't take care of nothin'." This from Nel, tugging on a long clean Camel, sitting up as if not to miss the show.

"Ah," Thurman says, "you don't wear them anyway—you too stubborn and too full of yourself...like without them extra pair of eyes you some right-on mama. I've seen you—don't think I haven't. Shakin' your stuff. Inviting trouble, that's what you been doin'. Why, in no time you be having boys sniffing around."

"Go ahead, sister, go ahead, now...tell him about the big ole white boy you been entertaining." Nel waves the cigarette in the air.

"He ain't sniffin' nothing. He's a boy from school."

"Who ain't really in school," Nel says.

Thurman is pacing back and forth between the two, hands to his ears. He stops in front of Marlene and brings his hands to her shoulders. "You start bringing boys here, the next thing you be telling us is you is pregnant. Knocked up silly. You be as no count as any whore on the street."

"Ha! Or any mama on the couch."

For a split-second Marlene has her wish. No one speaks. Or moves. It is as if a mysterious pause button has been pushed—until her mother's whimper creeps across the room bringing Thurman's hand hard against his sister's cheek.

Marlene laughs maniacally. "She just afraid the seed don't drop too far from the tree. You both afraid." She lifts out of the chair, pushes Thurman away, and stomps out. She walks to the room where she sleeps and turns on the light. There is nothing of beauty here, nothing worthy of a bedroom: a single bed with the mattress showing out from under an unfitted rumpled yellow sheet, a pillow too-long hugged, a dresser with missing drawers, and walls pure of anything suggesting life.

Marlene kneels down at the side of the bed, presses her hands together, and bends her head. "Dear God, keep our baby sister safe. Kiss her for me. And God, take care of Mama—an eye for an eye as Reverend says—so get to it. 'Night, Lord."

Marlene asks me if I believe in God. When I hesitate, she admits to sometimes doubting, but there are times she's pretty sure.

Occasionally, while visiting Marlene, I feel like I am watching a theater production of life on Georgia Street. Now the curtain rises. The ficus tree, the magazines, the floor swept clean. I resist the sense that things are out of kilter, that the story here is false. The story meant to reel me in, distract me from some truth. It is the dark side of Georgia Street, bursting with assorted comings and goings. Many times, I sense a swarm of others have skittered from the room, while all along—or for the six weeks she was living—baby Tina has been stashed from view.

Marlene's performance in seventh grade continues to fluctuate. Diligent one week, scatter-brained the next two. Over a year of weekly sessions of reading and writing, yet there is no sign I've made a difference. Now the voice inside my head repeats its command: Leave.

Fight or flight. The dichotomy of a response is telling. The first wave of survival passes and I am left with an urgency containing everything I claim to believe. Marlene's fate becomes the fate of what is possible, becomes the fate of meaningful change. Marlene may not know it—and certainly will never ask for it—but she still needs my help.

I decide, if nothing else, the least I can do is see about her glasses. And her tooth. With a missionary's fervor I spend the greater part of that year making my way through the state's health care system for minors. Marlene's family is on the Medicaid roll. Perhaps Thurman managed to get them signed up, then simply lost the will to persevere on his sister's behalf. I learn the names of agencies, as well as the importance of identification numbers, birth dates, and phone numbers. I sign the contact person line. Getting Marlene's vital information is as easy as asking. Nel supplies her daughter's Social Security number, her date of birth, and her insurance card. Nel turns it all over to me as easily as she handed me the picture of Marlene at five. I resisted then, and even now I fight the urge to hand it back.

I solicit the help of health care workers, as one mentor to another, and they respond. They teach me how to ask and answer the slew of questions it will take to assist Marlene. A Vanderbilt ophthalmologist, admitting he does not know how Marlene manages—in his opinion she is legally blind—secures paper work for federal assistance and introduces us to the optometrist who helps Marlene decide on not one but two different sets of frames that suit her. This works fine, until it doesn't. The dentist examines Marlene's tooth and, with eyes that hold no wonder, tells me if paper work had just been done, the tooth could have been extracted years ago. But I have lessons yet to learn. My self-assigned role as mentor only goes so far. New paper work demands a legal guardian's signature and presence at the time of surgery. "Ha! My mama will do it," Marlene says. I open my mouth to protest, but something stops me. Something in her voice, its tone—benevolent on my behalf. "Or Thurman. Thurman's off on Mondays."

"Fine," I say to the dentist, "we'll get back to you."

I am surprised at how easy it is to distance myself from Marlene. With the flurry of the end of spring semester, we spend less and less time together.

"Mrs. Merrick called me to her office," Marlene says, handing me the latest timed writing. "Asked if I might work in the library after school. Says it was your idea, says you told her I'd do fine."

"You will," I say, placing her paper in the rose-covered folder, which, full as it is, has managed to retain its shape.

Summer brings its own catalog of excuses: I am on vacation, or the Brooks's phone stays unplugged for days, or it's too hot. I send postcards from my travels and Marlene leaves "Hellos!" on my answering machine. It is not until that fall, her last year of middle school, I get a call that draws me back.

"Miss Ruth, I need your help."

She waits at the curb in front of Georgia Street, wearing short black boots and an off-white sweater dress that fits too well. She faces away from where she might expect to see me, and I have the sense she's ready to bolt. I drive up slowly, tap the horn, and see her shudder as she turns around. I shudder, too, wave through the windshield to keep my spirits up. I've spied the tooth, still tangled in her almost smile.

At the Dairy Dip, we eat our lunch outside. I realize I've been holding my breath when Marlene finally asks me if it's possible to get AIDS on your arm. I watch her pick the crust off her white bread bologna sandwich, discarding bits and pieces in a pile on the concrete picnic table. I used to do that, take the crust off white bread bologna sandwiches. Only I kept my crust intact, unwinding one long piece, which somehow never left the plate. I finish my cherry drink, then swirl the ice with my straw. Marlene pushes up her sleeve to uncover a patch of what looks like poison ivy. I laugh—out loud—and suggest we get some Benadryl. When she giggles, I recognize there's more to come. She-and-this-boy-were-playing-around-and-he-squirted-his-stuff-on-her-arm. Right here, Miss Ruth, she points as if I might not see. Right here.

Within days, we make our way to St. Thomas Family Clinic. I call ahead, explaining, as I learned to do, my role as a tutor/mentor from State trying to help a local middle school student. We meet Dr. Gwen. Surely older than she looks, with short hair, black slacks, and a soft-blue doctor's coat that matches the veins on the back of her hands, she asks to speak to Marlene alone.

Returning to the waiting room, I am grateful for the clean cool colors, the paintings of the sea, the cushioned chairs and couches. Around me, women wait. There is an air of exhaustion in the room. Hands rest in large laps, chins dip, heads rest against the wall. No one reads, or talks, or watches CNN. We rest.

Marlene comes to get me, and I cannot tell from looking at her what to expect. In the examining room, Dr. Gwen informs me Marlene agrees I should know her recent sexual relations have resulted in a full-blown case of herpes. Another curtain rises. I feel squeamish, like seeing roaches scatter on the stove. Only this time I can't escape.

Dr. Gwen's face is impassive, neither appalled nor sad, as she fills out the prescription pad. Marlene and I both listen to the regimen of applications needed to clear up this incident, for now. The virus will return of course, she will be susceptible all her life. Leaving, I corner Dr. Gwen for words of counsel. What now? Birth control? I ask, but Dr. Gwen has moved down the hall. She looks back at me and nods while knocking on another patient's door.

In the car driving to the drugstore, Marlene is sullen, but unapologetic. I feel as if I'm reaching across a canyon-like gorge, while from the other side, she skips along the edge. When she does talk, it is to ask if Thurman has to know. I sigh with the first sign of emotion either of us has let slip, then I follow her lead, and answer matter-of-factly no.

Thirteen-year-old girls must have their mother's permission to get the birth control patch. I do not want to talk of this with

Nel. My instinct tells me it will not be pleasant, and it isn't, but not for the reasons I fear.

I start out with the fact that Marlene has been sexually active. A titter escapes before Nel drops her eyes. I realize the only news here is that I am wise to her daughter's situation. When she raises her eyes, I catch a glimmer of delight before she starts bombarding me with tales of Marlene's interest in sex, how Nel dutifully related everything she knew about men's penises and what they want from women. She rambles on. To keep from covering my ears I stare at the empty TV screen. Needing her signature keeps me still, until I realize she has started in on Marlene, describing her body with foul words that make me blush. This is ugly. This is more than I can take. I drop the papers on the table and I leave.

It is two weeks before we return to Dr. Gwen. Nel has lost the permission papers but hand-writes a note and gives it to Marlene. I can only hope. I am now accustomed to this weight of dread, the dread that I will forget a vital something and we won't be able to proceed. And it will be my fault.

There are delays. Marlene has chlamydia, which Medicaid demands must be treated at the hospital. We begin to spend Tuesday and Thursday mornings before school at St. Thomas Hospital, where every hour prayers float from the PA system and no one seems to mind, including me.

Notations on my calendar show more than a dozen visits to either the hospital or clinic from January to February. A large "OK" fills a Friday in February block. I see us in the car, returning to school after Dr. Gwen has affixed the patch. To return Marlene by lunch, I take a shortcut down Post Road, past a gated community bursting with grand homes and immaculate landscaping. She is staring out the window. In all these weeks, with everything we've been through, I admit to the occasional blush and squeamish naiveté, but this morning it is the sight of Marlene in the shadow of such opulence that embarrasses me most.

"Those are some houses, huh?"

She doesn't answer, and I cannot see her face. I push for a response. "How do you think those people got in those houses?"

She turns in her seat and looks straight ahead. "Hard work," she says.

"You think? So, if you don't live in a house that large it's because you haven't worked hard enough?"

"People get lazy."

"I don't live there. Does that mean I'm lazy?"

"No. It just means you teach."

We both smile. It's been a long morning, but here we are at school, and if she hurries she can still make lunch.

The intensity is more than I can bear. I back away. Like Cammy in the nursing home, my heart is closing down. Though not completely. I will come home from class maybe two months later to find a message from Mrs. Brooks on my answering machine. Her voice moves like mud from the confines of a space I wish I'd not disturbed. "Bitch." "Dyke." The accusations come in slow, deep breaths. "White." "Pervert." A sharp pain twitches in my heart as I listen, over and over. The woman is drunk, or high. She doesn't know what she is saying. Still I flush, afraid of how my time with Marlene might be misconstrued.

It is always just the two of us. My mind races with Marlene's aversion to crowds, riding in the Civic, the drive-through restaurants, stopping in the park. And the shopping. We've bought jeans and shirts, of course, but it is the new swimsuits, bras, and panties I remember when the chilling claim of "pervert" strikes my ear.

I crouch on the carpet and sob. I hear my old professor's warning to all of us starry-eyed graduate students that teaching is an act of love and thus an act of courage. My face cools. I push the play button. "White...dyke...bitch...pervert." The taunts are real, true harbingers of harm no sane person would ignore.

I close my heart and listen as the air around me hums *here it is—your out*, and I agree.

Dear Miss Ruth,

My folder came today. Stuffed with writings from our time together. Thank you. I know how much you loved the roses.

You'd like this library too. Being a high school and all, it's big. My lucky self gets to work here now. Sometimes...like when I'm putting one of the very books we read back on the shelf, I think of you. Ha! It doesn't seem so long ago that I took your pencil and left without a thank you or good-bye. But you kept coming back—with books and pens. With fancy papers. You were there with your gentle face and smile. You were there with hope.

So, my shift is over and I'm sitting in this nice cushy library chair waiting for Thurman to pick me up. He never understood my moping—what did you expect, he yelled, then pushed me against the wall—shoved some sense into me is how he put it.

Ten minutes. Time's up.

Bye now. Marlene

PS I wonder if you kept your word, or if you read my writing. I hope you did.

Certain Kind of Mother

Three weeks into retirement from the university, I find I want a clean kitchen floor. I want the wood to sparkle and the corners to be seen. With no mop to my name, a PETA t-shirt is my tool of choice. I scrunch beside a pail of soapy water, eye-level with souvenirs of splats and spills. I dunk and wring and rub with fervor. The room sports a hefty scent of ammoniated Ivory when the last plank is wiped, and I twist around to rest against the wall. So, this is what it should look like. This floor. This kitchen floor. Won't Rosalie be pleased?

Or will she notice? My daughter hasn't been herself—worried, I assume, about the new job she has been offered with Children's Services, which I will encourage her to take, regardless of the travel. The girl's lucky to have a job, times being what they are. And travel, as perilous and unpleasant as she describes, is still a good thing. You cannot live your life fearing terrorists or chatty seatmates. Truth be told, I always dreamed I'd travel more than I have. But time passes, you make decisions, and suddenly it's your daughter's plans that hold the promise.

The promotion is a good thing, and she must not worry about me. I've lived alone for years since the divorce, and just because I'm retired doesn't mean I'm retiring. I hope she can tell from the way I've spiffed up the place that I'll be fine. Polished the kitchen table, cleared the lazy Susan of its junk, dusted my bookcases, and hung my Dr. Ruth Meyers placard on the wall. If cleanliness is next to godliness, Rosalie should be reassured. This might be as close as I ever get to the big guy.

At the sound of crunching gravel, I scoot myself off the floor and hop toward the back door, leaving toe prints in my wake.

"That driveway's a mess, Mom."

"It is, isn't it?"

Rosalie's kiss misses my cheek.

The chairs are stacked in the hallway, but she doesn't notice. By the time she's filled the tea kettle and set it on the stove, I've wiped the table clean and brought in two chairs.

"Mother." The kettle whistles. Rosalie sets two of my three Wedgwood china cups on the table and pours water over green tea bags. "Rodney and I…"

I pull a box of Fig Newtons from the pantry, then set it beside my tea. We concentrate on the act of sitting. She pulls thick auburn hair over half her face. "We're getting married," she says, sending a coquettish peek in my direction. "He's every crush I've ever had, rolled into one."

My heart bumps. Not the sappy kind of bump, but the jumpy kind. "Oh my." I tear the tab off the box of cookies and rip open the cellophane. "Does your dad know?" The question escapes, surprising me.

Rosalie unfurls against the ladder-back chair, which totters now on two back legs; her fingers barely reach the table's edge. One unplanned gesture—one wave of the hand—will upset the balance.

"That's the best part. Rodney actually went to the office and asked Dad if he could have my hand in marriage. Oh my god, can you believe it?"

The chair sways forward. She is upright now, both loafers on the floor.

"I'm sure your dad was impressed." My laugh feels like I'm trying to stay inside the lines of a gigantic coloring book.

"He offered Rodney a cigar."

"A bonding moment, I'm sure."

"Are you being snide?"

"Well, I guess it's too much to expect Rodney to ask me for permission." I'm stacking cookies, one atop the other.

Rosalie's chin glides back into a sudden pout. This familiar gesture calls my bluff.

"I'm merely trying to take it all in—I mean, don't you want to at least live with him awhile before you..."

"Mo-th-er!" She inserts syllables where none exist. "I will absolutely pretend you did not make that comment." She covers her ears. "I will assume you meant to ask about our plans. Our wedding plans."

My bumpy heart races. "Wedding plans at thirty-five? Aren't you past that stage?"

"Mother. Wanting a wedding isn't something you outgrow."

"No? But weddings are so...so...theatrical, you might as well put on a play."

"They do that, you know—wedding theaters—videos in high-definition."

"Save me."

"Mo-th-er—would you rather I elope?"

"Have you considered it?" There may be a lilt in my voice.

"What kind of mother wants her daughter to elope?"

"A wise one?"

Snap. I've gone too far. With a furious thrust of her arm, Rosalie flings all the Fig Newtons into the air; she is crying as

133

they crumble to the floor.

"Honey, stop. I'm teasing." I grab her arm.

"No, Mother, you're not." She jerks away. "This isn't one of those times you can sweep your snide remarks aside with 'I'm teasing.' You meant it." She shoves out from the table. "You'd rather I elope!"

She stomps across the room and out the door. As I march to the pantry and take out the broom, I hear her car spewing gravel. "Shit," I say aloud, looking at the figgy mess trampled into my floor. "What kind of mother indeed."

I am sweeping furiously when Mary Anne telephones.

"Isn't this just so exciting? Her father and I are simply thrilled!" She goes on and on until finally, casually, she mentions that "Belinda Gibbs does the best weddings in town."

I grip the broom. "Best weddings, huh? Please don't tell me there's a prize."

"Well, not exactly," Mary Anne says. "But you know, to some folks, a wedding is the defining event of a lifetime, and in Nashville a well-planned wedding says more about you than who your granddaddy was or where you went to school."

I think of my own wedding: the eight bridesmaids, the trumpet, and the doves. "Guess I'd hoped things had changed a bit since Dan and I were married," I say, tightening my lips against an irritated sigh. "Haven't folks wised up? If not to the marriage myth, at least to the wastefulness of high-stakes weddings." Too late I remember Dan and Mary Anne had invited three hundred of their closest friends and business associates to celebrate their union.

"Oh, honey," Mary Anne gushes all over my faux pas, "it will be fine. I know this isn't your thing, but I'll be glad to help. What with Danny's work, we've been to all kinds of weddings—and

I've kept every detail tucked away in my little brain, just in case the day ever came when our Rosalie found her charming Mr. Right."

Our Rosalie. I swallow the words, but they persist in upsetting my carefully constructed attitude toward Mary Anne. Our Rosalie. I pride myself on my divorce, on convincing Daniel of the benefits of mutual custody. And when he remarried, I championed the idea that with Mary Anne in her life, Rosalie would have one more person she could count on. One more resource, I liked to say. Like a plumber, or a hairdresser, or a good broom.

I manage a polite response and promise we'll be back in touch.

The kitchen holds the last light of day. I take the vodka from the freezer, pour a shot, and settle in at the table. The window offers a fading view of my undersized backyard, faint with promises of spring. After years of acre lots—Daniel's choice—this tiny plot of land still seems divine. No more yardmen or garden catalogs. A push mower and clay pots are all I need.

The wedding comes to mind. For Rosalie's sake, it must be a family affair. Face it, kiddo, I chide myself, Rosalie is the product of mutual custody—and this most certainly will be a mutual-custody wedding.

I take a sip of my drink, but by now the vodka's warm and hard to swallow.

That night I dream an empty bus is parked in my dilapidated drive. The passengers maneuver potholes and asphalt weeds to sit in folding chairs in my backyard. They face away from the house. I tie a silver scarf around my head and rush outside, but as I move to greet them, I realize I know no one. My heart constricts. I slide into the only empty chair at the end of one long row. I feel the strangers' eyes, but no one speaks. It starts to sprinkle, and without a word I know it's me they blame.

Rosalie doesn't come by the house for a week. She's called a couple of times, once to tell me they had set the date, and once to announce she made an appointment with the wedding planner, Belinda Gibbs. That was the call that convinced me I'd need pills.

As I drive home from the pharmacy, I glance in the rearview mirror and jab at my close-cropped curls. I like the gray, though Rosalie claims it looks cronish. I reach across to the passenger seat and rest my hand on the small white sack with the small white bottle—pills for the faint-hearted—tucked inside. The pills, with their promise of serenity, taunt me until I approach my house and Percy Warner Park across the road.

Years ago, after Rosalie found her own place, it was this park that convinced me to move to a smaller—or, Rosalie's word, hobbit—house with great big windows. The park seduced me with its views of new green growth in spring and roasted-pepper foliage in the fall. I flick a yearning glance in its direction.

Rosalie's car is parked in the driveway; I pull in and search my purse for my list. Not my list, actually, but Rosalie's. The list of what the mother-of-the-bride is supposed to do. I grab my purse, my pills, my list, and rush inside.

Rosalie is lolling on the futon, and I shake my head at the sight of a thirty-five-year-old, college-educated woman reading *Modern Bride*.

"So, you're back. Are we over our little tiff?" I say.

Rosalie sits up and swipes at her bangs with plum-colored nails. "Mother, I've finally found the right man, and you want us to run off."

"Promise me you won't become bridezilla—bridezilla with the purple nails!" I attempt a smile and tighten my grip on the sack. "Another bride's magazine?"

She motions me closer. Her smile is wistful as we huddle over the cover tableau of one more flawless bride in wedding white.

"Okay, Mom, let's get going. Mary Anne is picking us up."

"We're driving together?"

"We are. I do not have the time to go back and forth anymore. We're doing everything together."

Going back and forth: the keystone to mutual custody. From the time she was five, Rosalie bounced from my house to Dan's and back again. Each house had its Room-For-Rosalie. She slipped into one (with its bunk beds and stacks of books and clothes tossed on the floor) or the other (a double bed with starched pink shams and built-in shelves for Ken and Barbie) seemingly with ease.

"You did say we'd be doing things together, only I didn't think you'd carry it to extremes." I'd been a bit surprised at her demand. And ashamed. It must have been hard for her, growing up astride two different households. Harder than I can bear to imagine.

"Everything, Mother."

So be it. "Let me change," I say over my shoulder. I carry the sack into the bedroom, take out the pills, open my bureau drawer, and drop the vial in a nest of socks and scarves. Idling in front of the gaping drawer, my bus dream comes to mind. Then, as these things do, the silver scarf I wrapped around my head in the dream conjures up another scarf from a lifetime ago.

A single scarf, draped across my absent husband's bedside lamp. The scarf's smoky-blue silk swallowing the room, dissolving thoughts of where I was and with whom, replacing what was clean and crisp and fine with a kicked-off-cover, balled-up-sheet, and sweaty kind of space I knew I'd die for.

"Shit," I say aloud, shoving the drawer closed. This is not the retirement I hoped for. Like when a creek bed dries and you finally see the stones that caused the rapids, all my old decisions are rising up to taunt me. I force my shoulders back and head toward the closet.

By the time I change into a denim skirt and return to the living room, I have resolved that, for once, I'll try to be the kind of mother Rosalie needs. I will try, really I will, to care about flowers, engraved invitations, bridal registries, and gift bags for the out-of-towners. But I will not dye my hair. Or paint my nails.

"Ready?" Rosalie looks up.

I shrug a denim vest over my best white cotton shirt. I am not wearing makeup. "Yes," I say, trying to believe I am.

Mary Anne is dressed in a blue knit suit that brings out the gray sparkle in her carefully made-up eyes. Daniel's second wife is not a trophy, in the flashy showcase sense. Comfortably attractive, petite with rust blond hair and untarnished skin, she is a woman who carries herself well.

"Mary Anne!" I say, almost screeching.

"Ruth!" Mary Anne stretches her smile, as if hoping it might count as conversation.

"Let's go!" Rosalie insists, managing to hug Mary Anne and me simultaneously.

I step up and into the back seat of Mary Anne's Escalade. "Nice car," I say, feeling my face flush with the effort of my lie. Gas-guzzling SUVs are not nice.

"Isn't it great?" Mary Anne says. "We've been wanting a new car, and with the wedding and all, I figured now is the time."

Wedding talk makes me turn my attention out the window. At the stoplight I look down into the car beside us, where a young child is furiously tugging at car-seat straps. The teary-eyed girl jerks a pink hair barrette from her tuft of hair and throws it at the woman who is driving.

"Mary Anne and Dad are planting trees, too," Rosalie continues.

"We figure with all the company and parties, we might as well."

"Trees," I say, thinking Dan and Mary Anne's huge home could use a bit of green, something more than sodded grass. As the Escalade moves away from the light, I watch the woman in the car beside us twist around and slap the child with a hand small enough to cup a single cheek. "Now is the time," I manage to say.

The wedding planner's house is deceiving. Small ranch on a cul-de-sac of small ranches, but its inside smacks you with smells. Cotton-candy sweet, eucalyptus sharp, and heady lavender. We walk through the foyer beneath figurines of cats, hung like marionettes from a ceiling strung with tiny lights.

"Mary Anne, so nice to finally meet you. And you must be Rosalie." Belinda Gibbs's abundant hair bounces behind a head-band of fake fur, which appears to stake her face in place as well. Her skin is taut and shiny, with penciled perfect lips and rosy cheeks. She wears a diamond ring. A large diamond ring, I notice, while trying to decide if her colorless nails are chipped or chewed.

"And this is my mother, Ruth Meyers."

"A girl can never have too many mothers," the woman says. With a glancing, unfocused look, she swipes my outstretched hand with both of hers.

"You think?" My laugh is lost in the shuffle of chairs around an oversized pine table. Its centerpiece is a papier mâché giraffe which seems much too large.

"Now tell me, what do you envision?" Belinda Gibbs situates herself with pen and paper in the chair next to Mary Anne.

I lean, craning toward Belinda Gibbs. "It will be small—just family and a few friends," I offer.

"Though it has grown a bit," Rosalie corrects me.

"The wedding is at St. John's Church, the reception at the club," Mary Anne says.

"Your theme?" Belinda Gibbs's pen is poised.

I lean again. "Theme?"

"Her vision," the woman nods toward Rosalie. "Her dream—in technicolor."

"Oh!" Rosalie's head bobs. "I want pink."

"Pink. Pink in June is good. Baby soft or snappy hot?"

"Oh God, not pink," I hear myself say. "Pink is so...so derivative."

During the next long moment of silence, I study the giraffe's eyes. I decide they are moping.

Belinda Gibbs reaches across the table for a large leather photo album. "Look through this," she says, opening the book in front of Mary Anne. "These are just a few of the weddings I've produced."

"Why, there's Trisha Young and her mom," Mary Anne croons. "And Becky Bates, and..."

I slip on my glasses, but from where I sit, the album is a blur. Still, following Mary Anne's lead, I let go with several oohs and ahs. I am getting this fourth-wheel feeling. Belinda Gibbs's apple-seed eyes never once meet mine; only Rosalie and Mary Anne win the woman's gaze. When Belinda starts gushing over baby's breath with pink primrose, I slouch back in my chair and let the giddy talk proceed without me.

The afternoon stretches on. I sit silent and resigned, feeling as if I've somehow measured low on the mother meter. As if Belinda Gibbs suspects I do not have a maternal gene in my body and certainly won't have the wherewithal to be the mother of this bride. Mary Anne, however, has aced the test.

"So. I think I have everything I need for now," Belinda says. "I'll write this up and send an estimate to..." Her eyes are on Mary Anne.

"You should send it to me." I pull a smile in place.

"Mom and Dad are splitting the cost right down the middle." Rosalie makes a quick slashing gesture and adds, with a small laugh, "Kind of like they did with me."

Back at my house, Rosalie gets in her car, and I wave as she and Mary Anne drive away together. Above me, the sky is spiked with stiff, white clouds hurrying across the last of this long day. Still, there is time. I rush inside. My vest slips to the floor, and by the time I reach the hall closet, I've lifted the shirt over my head and unhooked my bra. I drop everything in a heap, step out of the skirt, and open the door. A pair of bicycle pants—shin length to cover warped veins—hangs from a hook on the wall. I study the crotch with its smooth, lambskin padding and hesitate just a bit before pulling off my underpants and pulling on the bike pants with unnecessary force.

The rest is easy. The sports bra, the back-pocket shirt, the shoes, and ankle socks with loony frogs. This is a side of me Daniel never knew—this energetic, sporty side. I only discovered it myself after the divorce. At first I jogged, then kayaked, but when the knees and shoulders gave out, I picked up biking. I've read that growing old gracefully really means adjusting to your body's disabilities. Making do. This bike, racing red with upright handlebars, is my adjustment.

I take the route that curls through the park, through familiar trees I have yet to identify by name. My pedal strokes are fluid, my arms relaxed as I approach the steepest incline with heart and breath in sync and gears adjusted. The trick is to balance slow with steady and think of other things—like pink wedding bouquets or hanging cats.

Or visions. I reach for my water bottle, keeping my sights on the climb before me. In the 1970s, the feminist vision was bandied about by women braver, more articulate than I. But I heard their call, read their words, and followed their lead. The lead of women willing to confront what was expected, willing to step outside the shadows of their men. It was a heady time, an angry time, but all the time my Rosalie kept me tethered, kept me real. I pedal hard, crest the hill, and wipe my forehead with the back of my hand. There is a quarter mile of flat and then I descend, forgetting to notice the view.

Two in the morning and someone is banging at the back door. Oh, god. I grab my housecoat and the heavy flashlight and stumble toward the ruckus before I recognize my daughter's version of a whine.

"It's me, it's me."

"Here, I'm here." I unchain the door.

"Why don't you have a doorbell, a simple doorbell? Would that be so difficult?" Rosalie moves past me to flip on the kitchen light. What I notice is the floor; the grime is back.

"Can we have tea? Or no. A drink. I want a drink." She is jerking open cabinet doors.

"I have some great pills," I offer, only half joking.

Rosalie holds up a bottle of amaretto. "No, this should do it."

"If you insist." I remove two small glasses from an open cabinet and set them on the table.

"I should have known. Jelly glasses." Rosalie pours the liqueur and sits down with a shaky sigh.

"Porky Pig and Daffy Duck are waiting at the bottom."

"Okay, let's drink up fast. Cheers!" Rosalie toasts. "Oh, how dare I? Now comes the part about you and your preference for cin-cin! Well, isn't it a bit pretentious—an Italian toast when you've never been to Italy?"

I sip, avoiding her hard gaze. She is baiting me, but the moment will pass. It always does, and then we get to what is true.

"Mom, I gave Binky to Rodney and...and...he laughed. He said it stank—it needed washing."

Binky, the beloved quilt my mother sewed for Rosalie when she was born. Years of traveling with her from house to house, then to the dorm, then on to her own apartment, have worn the appliqués of Snow White, Cinderella, and Briar Rose into faded figures curious and hard to name.

"Maybe it's time you let it go." I hope I look anything but worried.

She finishes her drink and pours another. "See, that's just it. I'm never adult enough for you."

"Rosalie..." I feel my own whine.

"Admit it! If you'd had your way, I'd be sporting Birkenstocks and hairy legs."

My resolve is slipping. "I wanted you to be strong."

"And manage my own life."

"Without guilt."

"Did it ever occur to you that a little guilt is not always a bad thing?"

"We're not talking a little guilt—we're talking guilt that comes from—"

"Church?"

"Well, yes. Church is certainly about guilt," I say, taking the bait, but jerking my hand in the air, palm forward, signaling stop.

"And marriage?"

"Depletes the self." I lower my palm and slap the table. "So there," I say with a weak laugh, "Dr. Meyers's lecture 101, the lullaby you've heard a hundred times."

"What kind of mother says that to a child?" Rosalie cries.

"I'm sorry, honey. I really am. I just wanted you to have a head start. If you knew what it took me so long to figure out, you could go from there. Not that you wouldn't make the same decisions—not that you wouldn't fall in love—but when you did, you'd be more…more informed."

"Informed? This is me—Rosalie—your daughter, not some student you're lecturing."

"I've made a mess of it," I say, searching my daughter's face. "A mess of mothering."

"Is this where I'm supposed to throw my arms around you? Where I'm supposed to tell you how I know anything you did, you did for love?"

"It's not really about me, is it?" I say softly.

Rosalie slumps down on the table, her head in her hands. "But don't you see, I'm like you in so many ways. I worry if I'm doing the right thing. I may not be the marrying type. I like my own place, my own routine, my way of being."

"But in just as many ways, you are not like me." My finger touches her single strand of early gray. "Admit it, you like the life of Mary Anne and your dad."

Rosalie tilts her head away from my reach. She stands and walks to the window's blank stare.

"I like the certainty of it," she says.

"But is it? Certain? I don't think so. Not much is. Even Mary Anne and your father are just leaning toward the light, hoping for the best."

"I want a good life."

"It will be."

"Even if it's different from yours?"

"We all have our own ideas of what the good life is—our private vision."

Rosalie's breath has collected on the pane. "There are these moments," she says softly. "Rodney and I can just be hanging out, when I catch his glance, and all I want to do is slip him on a silver spoon and swallow."

Peering down at Daffy Duck, I am silent with the weight of wanting to say something profound. Something motherly. "It is exciting," I manage.

"It's afraiding," Rosalie says. Her smile is suddenly giddy. She presses her finger to the pane and traces a lopsided heart.

Just before the cocktail supper at Dan and Mary Anne's, I return to my bureau drawer, force my hands to slither through the socks and scarves, and grab the pills. I swallow two.

In the sprawling group of well-wishers, I feel edgy. A whiff of drenched gardenias announces the short woman with gleaming teeth who clasps my hand. "Ruth, so good to see you," she says. "You've forgotten. I'm Lizzie."

I think back to the annotated guest list Rosalie left with me last week. "A cheat sheet, Mom—you already know a lot of these people—Mary Anne's friends you've met through the years." Rosalie suggested I study up, and now, with this woman preening before me, I wish I had.

"Lizzie," the woman peers over frameless glasses. "You know, dear, of Lizzie, Bitsy, and Mary Anne."

"Oh yes," I say, ready to hug her, "Mary Anne's Three Musketeers!"

"Yes indeedy…and speaking of Miss Bitsy…" As if on cue, a pixie of a woman glides over to us.

"We go back a long way—since kindergarten and Girls' Prep days," Bitsy pipes up.

"And you've managed to stay in touch?" I ask.

Lizzie blinks and blinks. "Oh, more than in touch. We are still best friends."

"Hm… My best friends from high school have all scattered," I say.

"How sad," Lizzie says.

"Sad? I like to think we've all gone on to new horizons." I am pleased with my swaggering tone.

Lizzie's eyes narrow. "Yes, that does seem to be a pattern of yours. Going on to new horizons…"

"But aren't we lucky," Bitsy adds. "Your new horizons left Danny free to find our Mary Anne!"

My face finds its grimace. "Your Mary Anne should thank me!"

"There you are." Rosalie slides her arm around my waist. "Isn't this the best party?"

"Yes, dear," Bitsy purrs. "Your mother was just telling us how grateful we should be that she decided to leave your father."

Rosalie cringes, loosening her proprietary grasp on my waist.

"Now wait a minute," I say with an empty laugh. "I tried to make a funny—Rosalie, sweetie, you know my sense of humor can be lacking."

"Don't you worry, dear. It doesn't matter," Bitsy says. "After all this time, what matters is you've finally found your man."

"Gracious, for a while there, we had our doubts," Lizzie says. "You just never dated any boy for very long."

My spine prickles. "Like the song says, behind every good woman is a string of good men!" This laugh is larger than intended. "Besides," I add, sensing my daughter's fury, "Rosalie has been very busy—with school and a career."

"Yes, you did get wrapped up." Lizzie pats Rosalie's shoulder, then grabs her hand.

"Almost like you were afraid to slow down. Afraid to commit," Bitsy commiserates.

"Maybe I was," Rosalie says softly. "I certainly had reasons…"

Together, Bitsy and Lizzie nod. "But here you are, our Rosalie, about to be a bride. We are beside ourselves!" Bitsy says, latching on to Rosalie's one free hand.

Seeing the three of them, their fingers entwined, my smile droops. I imagine a haunting chorus of red rover, red rover, let Ruth come over.

"Excuse me," I say, "while I run to the little girls' room."

I escape to the bar and lapse into brooding. Dan and Mary Anne's house is tasteful in an ordinary kind of way. Not my taste, of course, but certainly Daniel's, with all those heavy gold picture frames and candelabras. Lots of yellow chintz and oriental rugs, no drapes. It has a settled air about it. If Daniel and I had stayed together, our home might look like this. We'd bought a blue chintz couch. And a rug. A large Persian rug.

I ask for wine from the young black man tending bar. "Does it bother you to be the only person of color in this room?" I ask conspiringly.

"No, ma'am," he says, twisting a corkscrew deeper.

"It should," I say and take the drink he hands me.

The man gives me a futile glance and then steps away, as if from something harmful. I feel as if I've lost my only friend.

"Still fighting the good fight." Daniel stands beside me, a fuller version of his younger self. Confident, with happy eyes. The world, his world, always was a good and wholesome place. Before I can think of something clever to say, his elbow nudges mine, and he directs my attention across the crowd. Rosalie and Rodney have managed to find a quiet space. Daniel and I watch as our future son-in-law leans down and whispers to Rosalie. She beams.

"Remember the first time she went away to camp?" I say.

"She kept writing to us about wanting to make friends."

I nod. "And then she wrote about the girls…"

"Those hateful girls…"

"She didn't make a single friend."

Something passes between Daniel and me.

"I remember," he says, looking down at the carpeted rose beneath his polished wingtips.

I expect him to move on, take up his hosting duties. But he just stands, looking out over the crowd, until a man with a goatee and a plaid vest comes up and demands his attention. "Nice party you got going here, boss." The man raises his drink glass.

"Isn't it though?" I say before plunging back into the crowd, determined to mingle. I make my way from one cheery person to the next. My eyelids bat, my laughs are full, and, for a while, I suspect I am having fun. At some point it occurs to me I might be dreaming. Not one of my usual dreams. This dream I had years ago, when Daniel and I were first married. These friends, this house—if I had to name what it was I let loose of way back then, this was it. I lift a plate from the buffet table and help myself to caviar and shrimp.

Here was my dream, all grown up—a dream grown up without me.

It is late when I arrive home, kick off my boots, and snap on the kitchen light. A starkly utilitarian glare accompanies me to the sink, where I empty the pills down the garbage disposal and welcome its growl. The light is maddening. I turn it off and moonlight replaces it. I make my way into the living room, shove open the front windows, and fall in a heap onto the futon. The room whirls and with it my thoughts. The evening hadn't been that bad, really. As I threaded my way through the crowd of civilized, gracious guests, they mostly talked of the honored couple, or the weather, or told lame but not off-color jokes.

I turn on my side and bunch the pillow firmly against my cheek. Of course, no one mentioned my retirement, my biking, or that I participated in the March for Women's Lives. I try not to imagine the after-party chatter, but certainly my flowing aqua skirt and shiny boots would be fodder for those women all decked in black.

A chuckle escapes, then a disgusted sigh. I open my eyes. I am very awake. Wired, as Rosalie might say. Suddenly I miss the presence of a man. I rarely get tired of feeling free, but on a night like this, I waver, worried I'll be sorry at some end. The room begins to sway. I roll over, plant my feet on the floor, and sit upright. An owl's lone hoot makes its way from the park, and, outside, under the window, my single lilac bush smells more than grand.

For three days, I trek with Mary Anne and Rosalie to every bridal salon in Nashville. Each dress is lovely, but each one has its flaw. Rosalie doesn't like the sleeves, or the train, or the skirt. We move on.

The Dreams Galore boutique showcases Maria Castillo's personal creations.

"I don't want sleeves," Rosalie says.

"She wants a shorter train," Mary Anne says.

"And most of what we've seen is much too puffy," I add.

Maria listens with sketchbook in hand, and then her pencil flies across the page. She works for a full five minutes before holding up a replica of the very dress Rosalie has wished for all along.

"Yes!" we cry, grabbing hands and squeezing.

The month of April brushes past, though Nashville's sweet pastels fail to soothe my daughter's nerves. We are again in Mary Anne's car, driving to Maria's shop for the final fitting. From the backseat, I catch Mary Anne's glance in the rearview mirror. We are each anxious, mindful of what is at stake. "So, Mary Anne, I was thinking about your wedding dress—I remember bringing Rosalie to the church and you meeting her at the side door. Your mantilla veil was stunning."

"And the train with pearls—I thought it was the most beautiful dress ever made," Mary Anne sighs. "So, Ruth, tell us about your wedding dress."

"Well, if I can remember back that far, the empire waist had a blue sash, and I wore a Juliet cap entwined with blue ribbons."

"A blue theme," Mary Anne teases. "Beautiful!"

"You know, I offered my dress to Rosalie."

"Sorry, Mom, your wedding dress has bad karma. Besides, I want my own dress. My own beautiful dress," Rosalie says. "It's supposed to bring tears to my mother's eyes. That's a sure sign I've found the perfect dress."

"Well, we'll see." I am not a crier. I can hear my daddy now: "Bite the bullet, kid."

At the boutique, Maria ushers Rosalie away to the dressing room. Mary Anne and I sit flipping through still more bride magazines. I scan the pictures like I used to scan event programs as I'd wait for Rosalie's dance recital, or spelling bee, or forensic meet. The empty gesture hides not impatience, but dread.

When Rosalie was three, she ordered me "Away!" from the slide we always climbed together. I obliged and then could only watch as she pitched over the edge. The same feeling I had then comes to me now—of being impotent, unable to break the fall, of waiting for the certain crack of bone, the thud.

Mary Anne is giving me a gentle nudge. A rustle behind the curtain prepares me for Rosalie's entrance. But the woman here is not the bride of magazines or fashion shows. This bride pauses, veiled and bare-shouldered, in a cloud of tulle, Irish lace, and pearls, her face anything but vacuous or hollow. The glow from this bride's face makes me believe.

I cannot identify the emotion that propels me across the room, makes me take Rosalie in my arms, and crush her against my breast, squeezing with every ounce of mother I can muster.

"Careful!" Rosalie shrieks, then laughs, then pulls away to

set her veil on straight.

I step back. Mary Anne is crying now, in dainty sniffles. She hands me a tissue.

I dab at dry eyes and look at Rosalie—a grown-up with a dream. This moment, I realize, is of little consequence in the scheme of happy-ever-after or marching down the aisle to say I do. And yet, I smile. A mother's smile. Smug, and very good.

Rosalie stops by the house to drop off wedding proofs and surprises me with an impulsive hug. "Oh, Mom," she says, her face beaming, "being married is so much better than getting married!"

She leaves the proofs for me so I can take my time. Sorting through them is surprisingly difficult. In this one the camera seems to have pocketed my soul. My face is eerily transfixed beneath a smile forced from smothered fears. My arms are folded tight against my chest, holding all the journeys stuffed within. What the camera misses is the good life that is mine, culled from spirits broken, hearts I've left along the way.

I push away from the kitchen table. I've been hunched here long enough to lose the benefit of natural light. Reaching for the light switch, I'm waylaid by the window's view: my park at its full green best, a sky offering to swallow me in blue, an August heat shimmering its last hurrah. I jump up, rush to the closet, and change into biking clothes. It's been too long.

When I walk through the kitchen, I pass the table stacked with still unsorted proofs. A single photo stops me. Rosalie in her perfect dress, her father in his tuxedo finery, and me in blue silk. We are raising our glasses, and poof, the camera flash has caught our toast. The three of us strain forward, wide-eyed, looking—you might say—for our own kind of ever after. I lift the picture and prop it against the salt shaker in the middle of the lazy Susan, where I can see it even as I head out the back door.

Staying Alive

Rosalie is determined not to be the kind of tourist who looks at foreign landscapes through the lens of home. It is a breezeless Italian June along a raggedy two-lane road the concierge has assured her she could walk. She tries to focus on an overgrown meadow of sunflowers and ignore the adjacent field of hay spooled like bales in Tennessee. She feels a ghost-like breath against her ear, swats at empty air and, reminded why she's come, peeks over the rim of her sunglasses to get a fresher look at potential spots for Ruth's ashes.

Ruth. During those last months, Rosalie began to call her mother by her given name because she had insisted that it "elevated" the nature of their bond. Rosalie shakes her head, annoyed, even now, with her mother's peculiar ways. Rosalie is forty-three and barely slender, with her father's auburn hair and cheekbones her friends envied. She has taken time off from her job at Children's Services because she is her mother's only child.

She turns and kicks a piece of gravel up the hill, strides to where it lands and kicks again. She carries the box of ashes in her backpack, and as she hitches it over her shoulders, thinks it wasn't such a good idea. What with bits of bones, the box is heavy, and the pack presses hot against her cotton shirt. She will go only as far as the next town, have a bite of lunch, and then start out once again to spread the ashes.

Ruth died at seventy-one, before she had a right to. There were things Rosalie had meant to say, things her mother would have wanted to hear. Like how, now that she is ten years older than her mother was when she divorced her father, Rosalie gets it. Growing up within the confines of the Baltimore Catechism and Emily Post would tend to stunt a girl's perspective. Rosalie no longer cringes remembering how her mother talked of wide-awakeness or still becoming or quoted Simone de Beauvoir and Sartre decades after they had been in vogue. Though as a teenager, Rosalie would do more than cringe. She'd go and stay with Dad and Mary Anne.

Rosalie was eight when her dad remarried. Mary Anne drove an SUV, served dinner every night at six, and went to church. The everydayness of her father's household offered a reprieve from Ruth's antics. Rosalie stayed there more and more.

A motorcycle hurtles up the hill. She steps to the edge of the road. As the cycle whooshes by, its rider gives a gentle beep that makes her smile. She hesitates, then adjusts her pack and continues the climb, thinking, Christ, smiling at a stranger's beep. Incorrigible.

She shields her face with her hand and sees Pienza there, astride the one last hill. She walks faster now, but random memories persist. She was eleven or twelve when she asked her mother why she divorced Daddy. Unperturbed, Ruth explained. "For fifteen years, your father and I tried to be Mr. and Mrs. America. Then I took up consciousness-raising instead of bridge and wanted out."

Rosalie and her mother moved from a neighborhood of

endless yards and neighbors who would tell her when her mom was calling, to an apartment complex with two pools, a weight room, and no grass.

That's when Ruth started exercising. Not cycling yet. She was jogging back then. She'd laugh when telling how at first, because she saw herself as larger than the rest of the runners, she'd slip out at dawn and duck behind the hedge if someone passed.

Rosalie lay in bed and heard the soft shut of their front door. She remembers flopping on her back under the covers and listening to the kitchen clock—to the way it dripped instead of ticked as she lay still.

She crosses the road and walks beneath a humpbacked bridge into town. The climb is steeper here, as the concierge warned, but she sees the restaurant he suggested up ahead. Ruth wanted her daughter to learn to think for herself. "What do you think?" was her mother's mantra, even during those final days. Rosalie's insides tighten—a familiar feeling.

"Where they land is up to you," Ruth told her when Rosalie persisted in asking what she should do with her mother's ashes. "For me, there's no hereafter. This is it." Ruth drew herself up straight and slid her too-thin arm from under the covers. "Think of it as an adventure," she teased, reaching out, managing to touch the cuff of her daughter's tailored suit.

"For once, no riddles, Ruth. Ashes don't go bad. Answer me or I'll keep you in my sock drawer."

"Rigid till the end," Ruth sighed, then relented. "Someplace in the sun—the Tuscan sun. Damn, it was lovely." She lay back and glanced sideways at a photograph of herself with fellow cyclists, posing in front of an entrance sign to Capitoni Marco Vineyards in Pienza. She'd made it—after all those years—made it to Italy before she got so sick. Now she kept the photograph on her nightstand with the pills. "You know, honey," she said, looking back at Rosalie, "I would die for you, but I cannot live for you." Rosalie glared at the ceiling. The Ayn Rand quote was one she detested, but this time Ruth continued. "You're going to have to trust yourself to know the spot, but first you have to take the time and go."

Ristorante de Vista hugs the hill and offers terrace seating. Rosalie takes a seat inside, facing away from the chaotic kitchen, as her dad taught her. A boyish waiter approaches. She slips off her sunglasses and squints up at him as he begins to bow.

"Welcome, my lady," he says. "Too much outdoors? Your walk. It has made the inside seem more pleasant?" His smile lines crinkle and she suspects he is no boy.

"I did walk."

"Yes, and, as I hoped, you managed to come here."

She frowns.

"It is me," he says, "me on the motorcycle. I passed and you chose not to wave."

"I don't wave at just anyone."

"And why is that?"

"Excuse me, but I came to have a bite to eat."

He persists and says his name is Angelo. She struggles with Italian phrases learned from phone apps, but just the fact that she tries has its effect. He guides her through the menu and doesn't laugh when she orders gelato before she thinks about an entrée or a wine.

"You must try our pocket noodles full of pears or perhaps our bocconcini," he says.

"I'm in a hurry," she says.

"You Americans. Always rushing. Eating in minutes after thinking about it for hours. I have visited America. You watch

TV shows of gourmet cooking. You buy cookbooks. But you eat at fast food restaurants or microwave those dinners in a tray. Such a waste. You are indifferent to the art of eating."

"Indifferent? Even though we think about it all the time?"

"Ahhh…thinking and doing…thinking and experiencing are not the same. Indifference makes you…how do you say? Like stone, empty of emotion, free of what it is that makes for joy."

She is not indifferent to the dimple in his chin. Or the way his hands move with each word, fingers dancing loose and long. No ring. His hair is dyed a cartoon yellow, his eyes are marble gray.

Since divorcing Rodney, her history with men has been tangled. Sex is delicious, but she tends to spend her passion on the kids who are her job. If it wasn't for the aphrodisiac effect of getting a child safely through the system or finding just the perfect foster home, she doubts if she'd date at all. Once her therapist asked her why she chose the men she did. The sheddable kind.

The trattoria is quiet; her watch confirms it's way past lunch time. Angelo returns, brings a champagne glass of peach gelato ringed with chocolate slivers and biscotti. His white pants catch the sun and cause a glare that makes her swallow.

"We are slow today," he says. "You will take your time, and I should join you? On your way to…"

"To Capitoni Marco Vineyards," she hears herself say as he turns, retreating to the kitchen with a nod.

She reaches for the spoon he's placed in the shadow of the glass, scoops a bite of cool sweet cream, slides it on her tongue, and wants some more.

Around her, the afternoon sun glances off a wall strung with photographs of happy faces. She shifts in her seat and feels the backpack resting against her leg. According to Ruth, her Granny Roslyn used to hang photographs of all their relatives on her bedroom wall. She'd hung that sad old family tree there too—before it ended up in the suitcase now stored in Rosalie's back room. Angelo is waving from across the way. Rosalie welcomes the distraction and smiles back.

"Italian driving is furious and fast, a splendid way to rush toward some place special," Angelo assures her.

"We'll see. It may not be a special place at all," she says, collecting her backpack and following him out the door.

An hour later, they are speeding out of town, the backpack squeezed between them on his Viper. She likes the way he doesn't pry, even after they've followed a haphazard road and approached a sign for Capitoni Marco Vineyards and she's shouted, "Stop!"

Capitoni Marco Vineyards, sponsor of her mother's race. Not just a race, a voice inside her head seems to scold. Your mother biked a century. That's what she called it when she rode a hundred miles, at age sixty-five. Though it took her several days, and she'd had to walk towards the end, Ruth always claimed she'd biked the distance.

Rosalie hadn't made an issue of it. Truth be told, at the time, she thought the whole thing rather foolish. Mary Anne and Dad agreed.

Rosalie rubs the backpack strap. The wind slaps against her cheek as the Viper races over dried-out pavement, bouncing through potholes Ruth might have come across as well.

The winery's collage of stone has held its own for longer than

Rosalie cares to know; its vineyards reek of ripeness and stretch in ordered rows like corn in Tennessee. Cars crowd the parking lot, but Angelo finds a place beneath a lemon tree, which shades a bench.

"My mother's ashes," Rosalie blurts out, placing the pack on the bench and stepping back.

"This is why you rush?"

"Maybe I should spread them here and just be done."

"Of course," he says, hesitating. "Though you could have spread them long before, and you have not. Perhaps the—as you say—doing of it, is tricky."

Rosalie leans against the tree; jet lag is catching up with her. "Thank you, kind sir." Suddenly reaching down to where he sits on the bench, she grabs his hand. "For the ride." She squeezes hard and lets go. Angelo is silent as she snatches up the backpack and walks away.

Alone, wandering through the groves, she almost smiles. Ruth posed here, celebrating with her friends. Rosalie thinks again of the photograph beside her mother's bed—it wasn't very good. Four women, arms entwined, their faces blurred but happy. The photo also failed to capture all these rows and rows of vines, profuse from tending.

Granny Roslyn comes to mind. Dead for over twenty years, she'd been the gardener of the family. Always tending, working in her beds even when she couldn't remember the flowers' names. Rosalie hugs the backpack to her chest, then zips it open and lifts out a plain brown cardboard box. Sprinkling the ashes, she recalls how Granny used composted coffee grounds, egg shells, and orange peels to fertilize her precious plants. She'd understood the value of returning the spoils of the earth home to the earth. A sort of hereafter—a version her mother might approve.

The sun is setting when she returns to the villa to find Angelo sitting on the bench with an uneasy smile. She isn't surprised. She is used to men showing their concern, and when they do, she knows to pull away. But tonight an accordion is playing.

"We are in luck, my friend," Angelo says, flashing a grin. "It is the sagra della vino, celebrating wines coming into season. The dining has begun, the dancing's started!"

Angelo ushers her through the banquet hall, past deserted tables spread with food-filled platters to an anteroom where music blares and the circled crowd is wildly clapping. Two women dancing in the middle of the room have brought the cheering patrons to their feet.

Angelo and Rosalie wedge closer. "Non capisco," she shouts, "I don't understand."

"Mrs. Brunelli and her daughter visit every year from Rome," a man beside her responds, nodding toward the women. One is gray-bunned, shawled, and flat-soled, the other henna brown and strapless, wearing heels. Rosalie watches as mother and daughter, fingers intertwined, turn inward and outward, entering, leaving, and returning to each other's space. Their eyes lock in mutual agreement, as if to look away will break their spell.

Rosalie's mother was a dancer. Ruth cleaned house to the music of the Bee Gees. "Come here and dance with me." With broom in hand, she hugged her grown-up daughter close.

"Turn it down," Rosalie wailed as she wriggled free.

Her protests made her mother more determined. When Rosalie rushed out the door, Ruth was breaking into a frenzy of dusting, belting out a chorus of "Staying Alive."

Rosalie quits her clapping to adjust the now lightweight backpack one more time. Mrs. Brunelli is not smiling. Sweat dots her flat-lined lips and stiffened jaws. A quote comes to mind, one that Ruth shared some time ago: "Raising a daughter is like living with a needle in your heart."

Rosalie feels herself give way. As if fingers have lovingly unbuttoned a tight coat, something inside her loosens. Something that enables her to give Angelo a hug then walk across the floor alone. This dance is hers.

She taps the women's shoulders and they catch her in their arms. As she loops around the room with Mrs. Brunelli and her daughter, Rosalie welcomes the ghostly breath of air soft against her ear. Her mother died before she had a right to. Rosalie wasn't done. Had she told her mother that she loved her? She is jolted by the memory of celebrating what Ruth called unbirthdays. Pouring sugar water from a china teapot. Serving saltine crackers on tiny metal plates. Rosalie gave her mother presents: a comb, a book, a tube of lipstick, all taken from Ruth's room. Now Rosalie blinks. Hard. They wanted so much from one another, and yet they grew apart. A disappointment, one to the other.

And yet. Those gifts—the comb, book, and tube of lipstick—she'd wrap each one in its own paper bag, each one decorated with carefully crayoned hearts, scribbled with what her mother claimed was the best gift of all, the words "I love you." Rosalie twirls and lets the memory seep in.

Notes of Gratitude

I'm grateful to be a part of two outstanding writing groups. Thanks to Nashville Writers Alliance members Rita Bourke, John Bridges, Ed Cromer, Phyllis Gobbell, Doug Jones, Will Maguire, Rick Romfh, Corabel Shofner, Shannon Thurman, and Jack Wallace. Your critiques and support have been invaluable. Much appreciation to my ever-faithful Dunn Writers Mary M. Buckner, Mary Helen Clarke, Carole Stice, and Ava Weiner. You nurture my craft, my spirit, and my horizons.

On the publishing side I am fortunate to have the amazing Nora Gaskin of Lystra Books and Kelly Prelipp Lojk of Lojk Design in my corner. Nora's keen insight and sense of story helped make *Fate Havens* a coherent reality. Kelly's artful sensibilities made it beautiful. I am indebted to you both.

Special thanks to my longtime nonwriting friends Jane Jeffords, Mona Lee, and Yvonne Hobbs. Our long-distance happy hours, playdates, and endless lunches keep me sane.

To Karen Essex for unending support and grounding, I am forever grateful.

To Joe DeGross, who taught and challenged me, you are missed.

Heartfelt thanks to family members Chrissy Havens Spigel, step-daughter and friend; loyal siblings Gini, Lisa, and Clif Dunn; and to my daughter Katie Hammer Johnson, who swears she's my biggest fan.

Loving gratitude to my husband and soul mate Barry Havens. Thank you for honoring the stories you knew were there.

Finally, thanks to my grandkids Thomas, Lucy, Nathan, and Ava, who've opened an unexpected chamber in my heart and made it impossible to say no. Ultimately *Fate Havens* is the result of their insistence that I write a book—a real book—a library book.

Made in the USA
Columbia, SC
11 December 2019

84700597R00105